Also by Jeffrey Shaffer

I'm Right Here, Fish-Cake

It Came With the House

Conversation Pieces
by Jeffrey Shaffer

With Drawings
by Paul Hoffman

CATBIRD PRESS

CATBIRD PRESS
16 Windsor Road, North Haven, CT 06473
800-360-2391; catbird@pipeline.com

Our books are distributed by
Independent Publishers Group

Library of Congress Cataloging-in-Publication Data

Shaffer, Jeffrey, 1953-
It came with the house : conversation pieces /
by Jeffrey Shaffer ; with drawings by Paul Hoffman.
— 1st ed.
ISBN 0-945774-36-2 (alk. paper)
I. Hoffman, Paul, 1950-   . II. Title
PS3569.H2985I87 1997
813'.54—dc21   97-14172 CIP

Contents

Night Caller

The jangling of the phone woke me out of a sound sleep. I snorted groggily as I put the receiver to my ear.

"The President's plane is missing!" said a frantic voice.

"Oh my God!" I answered, sitting bolt upright. The clock on the night stand said it was 4:15 A.M. "Who is this?" I asked.

"Hey, wait a second," said the voice. "Did I dial 683-2751? In Bethesda?"

"Not quite," I answered. "You reversed the last two digits."

"Damn!" There was a pause. "Look," said the voice, "could you go back to sleep and forget this happened? I need to make another call right away."

"It's a little late for that, pal," I said. "How could you screw up on something this important?"

"It's not my regular duty. I'm covering for a buddy tonight."

"Sounds like your sergeant's stripes are in jeopardy," I said.

"Sir," the voice answered angrily, "I am a three-star general! You think we'd entrust this crucial job to a lowly enlisted man?"

"I'm sorry," I said. "You sound very young, that's all."

"That is because I keep myself in peak physical condition," said the voice. "I don't hang out in smoky nightclubs listening to drug-addicted horn players and their devil music."

"Well, I can't just go away," I said. "If the President's plane is really missing, it could mean we're on the brink of a national emergency. Nuclear holocaust."

"Oh, come *on!*" said the voice. "The Cold War is over.

Who's gonna launch a nuclear strike against us these days? Burma?"

"It doesn't matter who fires the first missile," I pointed out. "This sounds like a good time to get my family down into the fallout shelter, at least until things settle down."

"You still have a fallout shelter?" The voice quivered slightly, as if the caller were suppressing a giggle.

"It came with the house," I said. "But the previous owner kept it well maintained."

"Look, mister," said the voice, "I got news for you. That little crash pad in your basement is a joke. It'd be like living in a septic tank."

"Oh, not at all," I said. "It's a nice shelter. Very roomy. It even has wall-to-wall carpeting."

"It's still gonna stink like a cowbarn after two days," the voice said. "The only way to do a fallout shelter is large-scale."

"Oh, like the big one at White Sulphur Springs, West Virginia? Is that where you're calling from?"

"Actually," said the voice, "White Sulphur Springs was for the slopeheads in Congress to hide out. Our shelters are even better. We got air conditioning, food service, jogging track. Hot-and-cold running girls. Ha! Just kidding about that part."

"You know," I said, getting a bit irritated by his attitude, "if I wanted to, I could hang up and call the news media about this. My next door neighbor works for CNN."

"Well, I'm about to hang up and deny I ever spoke with you," said the voice. "How are you gonna prove this conversation ever took place?"

"Because it's all being taped," I said. "I've been getting some prank calls lately, so I have a voice-activated recorder hooked up to this line. And you're coming in loud and clear."

"Damn!" There was another pause. "I bet you're lying," said the voice.

"Can you afford to take that chance?"

"All right. Tell ya what I'm gonna do. I got a lieutenant workin' in this department who does the best auto detailing you'll ever see in the mid-Atlantic region. How about you just forget we ever talked, and I'll send him over tomorrow to clean up your Toyota Land Cruiser."

"Why do you think I own a Land Cruiser?"

"I put a trace on the phone line a minute ago, and when we got your address I just swung one of our spy satellites into position fifty miles above your house. Oh, wait! That's not *your* driveway I'm lookin' at. Your car must be. . ."

"The Jeep Cherokee wagon," I said. "The Land Cruiser belongs to Bledsoe, my neighbor."

"Right, there we go," said the voice. "Hmm, for a second there I thought you had a little Jesus stuck on the dashboard, but now I can't quite make out who it is. Little bug-eyed bald man."

"That's a magnetic figurine of Homer Simpson," I said. "My daughter gave it to me for a birthday present."

"Who the dickens is Homer Simpson?"

"Don't you watch TV?" I asked.

"Not since my son went off to college. Say, is *Marcus Welby* still on?"

"I'm afraid not."

"Too bad. That was a hell of a show. And Robert Wagner, why, he was a role model for all of us."

"I think you mean Robert Young," I corrected.

"Yeah, the white-haired guy. He had class. Not like the punks on TV now. They just take their clothes off and grunt."

"Not to change the subject," I said, "but what do you think'll happen when people hear the President is missing?"

"Hold on a second." I could hear a muffled sound, like somebody's hand was covering the receiver. "Good news," said the voice a moment later. "We've got the plane back on radar. Some kinda interference in the upper atmosphere. All clear now."

"Tell me," I said, "who were you trying to call? I suppose the Vice-President is the first one to be notified."

"Yeah, right," said the voice, "and you probably still believe in the Easter bunny. Look, zip your lips and my detail man will be at your place at 8 A.M. sharp. Don't ask him any questions, though. Officially, he doesn't even exist."

"Wait a minute," I said. "This sounds somewhat sinister. Are you military people engaged in a conspiracy to keep the Vice-President from assuming the role of Commander-in-Chief under the provisions of the twenty-fifth amendment to the Constitution?"

"You really think old Bubble-Top could handle the job? He makes Bozo the Clown look like Nobel-prize material."

"That's very disrespectful!" I admonished. "Aren't you the least bit concerned that I'm recording all of this?"

"Actually," said the voice, "I've been testing the phone line with sophisticated electronic scanners, and there's no indication that any recording device is being operated."

"Oh, the tape is running," I said emphatically. "You can count on that, for sure."

"Why, looky there! Your voice just hit a spike on our audio analyzer, which is a good indication that you're not being truthful. I have a feeling this discussion is over."

"Okay, fine, I made up the stuff about the tape recorder," I admitted. "But wasn't that pretty quick thinking on my part?"

"Yeah, you got a point," said the voice. "Tell you what.

Since we did give you kind of a jolt, I'll let you have the car detailed anyway. Just 'cause I'm a nice person."

For some reason, I felt very tired after he hung up, totally stressed, and I promptly nodded off to sleep. When I woke up around noon, I poked my head out the bedroom window and saw Bledsoe standing next to his Land Cruiser. It was gleaming in the bright sunshine.

"An Army lieutenant showed up at eight o'clock this morning and detailed my car for free!" he exclaimed. "Who says the government never does anything right?!"

The Human Factor

I could see the woman approaching my secret cave headquarters from a distance. She was clearly visible on my security monitor: tall and athletic, dark-haired, quite attractive. For an Earth female, I should add.

"Hello? Is anyone in here?" She seemed unafraid as she called out into the forbidding silence of my hiding place.

"Elvira Mattingly. COME ON DOWN!" I bellowed. She jumped back in astonishment as I activated the neon energizers and filled the main room with a pulsing reddish glow.

"Oh my Lord!" she exclaimed. "You're a huge, free-floating brain creature!"

"Don't be too frightened," I said. "Actually, I've assumed the form of a large brain because it elicits a subconscious fear of the unknown and a respect for higher intelligence. It's like your great American president Knute Rockne once said: 'Make your opponents fear you, and respect you.' I like that."

"Knute Rockne was never President," she said, shaking her head emphatically. "He was the football coach at Notre Dame."

"Close enough," I conceded. "Now, Elvira, tell me a little about yourself. Where are you from?"

"I live in Beaverton," she said, "but I'm originally from Astoria. Oh, let's skip the happy talk. If you know my name, then you're obviously reading my mind. But your voice *does* have a familiar quality. It's putting me at ease right now."

"I learned English by listening to your primitive radio broadcasts and TV shows," I said. "After experimenting with

several different speech patterns, I felt most comfortable imitating Bob Barker on *The Price Is Right*. He seems to connect with his audience on a truly visceral level."

"That's discouraging," she said. "You must have a pretty low opinion of humanity, based on what you've seen."

"Not at all," I answered. "For example, *The Beverly Hillbillies* and *Fresh Prince of Bel-Air* both focus on the positive effects of moving to a better neighborhood. Such an advanced idea is quite uncommon on most planets I've visited."

"Do you have a name?" she inquired.

"On my own world I am called Zarkon 77," I explained. "But you can call me Zark if you'd like. I assume you found my cave by following your husband on one of his nocturnal visits here."

"Yes, we need to talk about my husband," she agreed.

I flipped a switch, and a moment later one of the viewing screens lit up with the image of a handsome man wearing a white lab coat. He was sitting at a bench, looking into a microscope.

"There's Clifton, working hard as usual," I said. "My scanner is tuned to his body's electronic frequency, so I can watch him all the time and make sure he is doing my bidding. I'm not really telepathic at all. I got your name from spying on Cliff at home."

"I knew he was being controlled by something," Elvira said. "He started acting differently about six months ago. So did he just wander in here by accident, or what?"

"I used to trap my subjects up on the surface by having them sink into a vat of quicksand. It was a wonderfully dramatic procedure, but not very discreet. Now I use a more psychological approach. When I'm targeting men, I just tie a string to a bag

14

of golf clubs and set it outside the cave entrance. It's like luring flies into a jar of honey."

"That's remarkable," Elvira said. "I don't think Clifton has ever played golf in his life."

"Doesn't matter," I said. "There's something about the clubs they can't resist. It's unique to your race."

"So how did you get him under your control?" she asked. "Did you create a duplicate Clifton inside a seed pod, like in *Invasion of the Body Snatchers?* Or is there some device you implanted into his brain?"

"The implant," I said. "It looks like a little tiny needle, inserted behind his right ear."

"That's what I thought," she nodded. "It took away all his emotions toward me, right? Like he was zombie-fied."

"Yes, exactly," I said. "It was unavoidable."

She looked back toward the viewing screen. Just then, Clifton took off his lab coat, lay down on the floor, and began doing one-handed push-ups.

"He can do those for hours now," Elvira said. "He never used to exercise at all. Is that something you planned?"

"Not really," I admitted. "Actually, the brain-control device has slipped out of adjustment recently. It doesn't interfere with my plans, but I guess it's been confusing for you. However, your husband is not totally devoid of feelings or motivation. "

"I'm not here to complain," she said. "In fact, some of the changes have been pleasantly surprising, like his new fascination with Cajun food and curry dishes. He's pretty much taken over the kitchen entirely."

"That's certainly a nice benefit," I said, "especially since he's going to be under my domination for quite awhile. I hope you weren't planning to plead for his release from my device."

"Oh no," she replied. "You see, this may sound odd, but

Clifton and I weren't doing too well before you came into the picture. We were both on the rebound when we got married. We sort of rushed into it. Things had been getting pretty rocky."

"Are you saying you're happier now that Clifton is my slave?" I asked, puzzled.

"Let's just say this is working out pretty good for me," she answered. "I've got this, er, friend I've been seeing. And he doesn't really want any commitment, which is fine. I don't want a divorce if I can avoid it. Clifton's salary and job benefits are fabulous. So now that his emotions for me are gone, I don't have to worry about him getting jealous. I just wondered how long it could go on this way."

"Eventually the situation will change," I said. "My superiors *do* have something in mind for your planet."

"I figured that," she said. "So, can you tell me how much time I've got to enjoy my new, carefree lifestyle before — well, what's your final goal? Invasion? Destruction of our environment so you can take over the world?"

"I honestly have no idea. Those decisions are classified," I said. "I'm just a mid-level functionary in this operation."

"I know that Clifton has been bringing you packages of steak and cans of gasoline for the past few months."

"Yes, I was instructed to collect data on food and fuel," I said. "But someone else analyzes all the information later. And as for how long this will go on, all I can say is we've been observing you for several decades. I'm actually set to be rotated back home, but my replacement hasn't shown up. He's three years overdue right now, so there may be a problem I don't know about."

"Can't you just call your planet?" she asked.

"Not a chance!" I exclaimed. "I mean, you never know who's eavesdropping these days. I have it on good authority that at least three other extra-terrestrial societies are snooping around this solar system. No, I just have to wait until someone shows up, and then I'll carry all the data back home personally."

"So, what you're saying is, I might have a lot of really good years ahead of me," she mused. "I was worried that, with everything looking up for me, it would all crash down soon. You ever get that feeling?"

"No, I don't," I said. "But since I have developed great empathy for you during this conversation, let me warn you about something. You know how I said my brain control device was a little out of adjustment?"

"Yes," she said, sounding uneasy.

"Well, there's another problem. The needle I stuck into your husband's brain is supposed to be permanent. But it may come loose and fall out after awhile."

"You're kidding!" She was definitely irked. "You can travel across space, but you can't make a brain implant that works right?"

"The whole machine was supposed to get serviced when my replacement arrived," I said, "so the maintenance schedule is all goofed up now. To be perfectly honest, the man I enslaved prior to your husband lasted about 18 months before the needle came out. Luckily he didn't die, but he did undergo some additional personality changes. He's now a very successful televangelist."

"No!" she said. "I will not let *that* happen. What can I do to make sure he stays under your control?"

"Avoid all contact sports," I recommended. "Especially roller hockey. And try to get him to wear a plastic cap on his head in the shower. Just make sure it covers his ears."

"I'll do the best I can," she said. "He seems pretty docile, but once in awhile he gets a little feisty."

On the video screen, Clifton had finished his push-ups and was lighting a small cigar.

"Now that's a new one," Elvira said. "He's never smoked since I've known him."

"He does now," I said. "Macanudos. They're not bad."

"Look," said Elvira, "I am giving you my sworn oath that I won't say anything about this. Can you at least let me know when your replacement gets here, in case he wants to change things?"

"Well, I can't promise," I said, "but yes, I'll try and tip you off. Anyway, for all I know, I could be stuck here for a good long time."

"Do you think your replacement had an accident?"

"Maybe. Or the bureaucrats back home may have cut off funding for this whole project. The budget battles are always a total pain in the you-know-where."

"So how long can you just keep waiting?" she asked.

"I won't get worried for at least another century," I said. "Our life spans are far longer than yours. And it's never boring either, especially here in Oregon. The whole micro-brewery trend has been amazing to watch. And I can tell you from personal experience that in this part of the galaxy there is nothing that tastes as good as cask-conditioned marionberry lager."

"I should go," she said. "It's going to be dark soon, and I won't be able to find my car. But, I was wondering . . . would you mind if I, well, touched you? I'm just, I've always been a very physical person."

"Be careful," I said. "Our body temperatures are a lot higher than you're used to."

Well, her fingers practically sent sparks flying when we made contact. Nothing like that has ever happened to me. After she left, I couldn't concentrate on anything. I know it's against regulations, but I'm going to phone her. Maybe she'll brush me off, but I don't think so. I have a good feeling. I think she's probably waiting for my call.

The Beat Goes On

Stagehands were milling around nervously in the hallway outside the dressing room, but as I approached they stood aside and let me pound on the door. It opened a crack, and I saw the frightened eyes of Blake, the concert promoter, staring out at me.

"Are you a doctor?!" he asked frantically. I pushed my way inside and slammed the door behind me. The air was warm and humid, and the entire room reeked of beer and sweat.

"Where is he?" I asked, and Blake pointed toward a cot against the opposite wall. Lying there before me was the limp form of Argo Skrull, founder and lead guitarist of Dysfunctional Utah, a band known for its techno-pop rhythms and complex vocal interplay. Almost two thousand fans were waiting for the group to make its appearance onstage, but Argo's condition did not bode well.

"I asked if you were a doctor!" Blake repeated.

"I'm his personal coach," I said, "and I'm the one who decides what we need." Argo was pale, and his skin felt clammy. I looked over and saw Freida Skye, the svelte blond bass player, standing in a corner. "Did you see what happened?" I asked.

"He seemed fine," she replied. "We split a can of Black Dog Ale, started to go over the list of songs for the first set, and then he just sort of drifted out cold."

"Argo!" I said loudly, shaking him by the shoulders. "Can you hear me? What's the opening song?"

His eyes didn't open, but his lips moved, and he suddenly blurted out, "Roll the Joe-Boys! Roll the Joe-Boys!"

"What the hell is he saying?" Blake asked. "I never heard them play a song with that title."

"This is bad," I said.

"Johnny don't sweat! He's every girl's pet!" Argo moaned, and then he curled into the fetal position.

"He's doing it again, isn't he?" Freida said.

"Doing what?" Blake demanded. "Did he take something? I got a stomach pump in my office, if that's what you mean."

"This is not an overdose," I explained. "'Roll the Joe-Boys' and 'Johnny Don't Sweat' are songs that Argo wrote when he was with a group called Toys in Babeland. They did catchy surf-style tunes with dark, edgy lyrics."

"Didn't that group dissolve years ago?" Blake asked.

"That's our problem here," I said. "Argo has a serious case of Band Regression Disorder."

"Say *what*?"

"You better get used to it, Blake!" I said. "B-R-D is starting to show up all over the country. Musical trends and tastes are changing faster than ever. Rock groups used to stay together for years. Nowadays a band will form, write some songs, develop a style, break up, re-group, merge with other bands, break up again. It happens so quickly that, in certain cases, the human brain cannot assimilate all the changes and variations."

"Oh God," Blake said, "this is not what I need. Is he gonna come out of it soon? Like right away?"

"I don't know. If it's just a light regression, we might be able to snap him back in a few minutes." I grabbed Argo by the shoulders and tried to lift him into a sitting position. His eyes were still clamped shut. "Argo, are you there? It's party time!"

His body suddenly jerked as if it had been jolted with an electric current. "Dude, you are rude!" he cried out, and then he leaped off the cot. I grabbed him round the waist, but he

dragged me across the floor and crashed head-first into a wall.
"Totally rude dudes!" he repeated, banging the wall with his
knees and elbows.

"I think he's having a petit mal!" Blake exclaimed.

"It's not a seizure," I said, "it's part of an onstage routine
he used to perform with Urine Tipped Arrows. They were a
neo-punk quartet that featured lots of slashing guitar solos."

Argo broke away from me with a grunt and fell on the
floor, writhing and flexing his back like a bloated python. His
eyes were still closed tightly.

"I've seen him do that before!" Freida said. "It happens
sometimes when we watch *NBC Nightly News*. The sound of
Tom Brokaw's voice can throw him into an altered state."

"That's the Sandsnake Shiver, a dance style he invented
spontaneously one night when he was a member of Jihad Beach
Party. They liked to rearrange old Bob Dylan songs into wall-of-
sound riffs with a driving disco beat."

"Can't you just give him a hard kick in the head or something?" Blake asked.

"You would have been a great help in the Middle Ages," I
said. "Fortunately, we have more sophisticated methods now." I
reached down and pinned Argo to the floor. Suddenly his eyes
popped open. I pushed his head so he could see Freida. "Argo!
Who is that?" I shouted into his ear. His eyes seemed to glimmer
for an instant.

"Astrid!" he said. "My Astrid is here!"

"He's awake, right?" Blake said, sounding hopeful.

"Not quite," I said, "but he *is* responding to visual images.
Astrid was the lead vocalist for Leatherette Barbie. That was
Argo's attempt at fusing industrial/art-rock with digital sound
manipulation, along with some Latin undertones."

"Astrid was my roommate for a year," Freida said. "She's

the one who introduced me to Argo. And I know all the Leatherette Barbie songs. Maybe we should just go out and start playing them."

"That *was* a great band," I said, turning to Blake. "What do you say? The crowd might go for it, don't you think?"

"If this was a junior high sockhop in Pismo Beach, California, they might," he said, almost sneering. "But we're in Seattle, with a packed house full of people who spend their time on the cutting edge of this scene. They paid twenty-five a ticket, and they're here to see Dysfunctional Utah!"

"The only thing left," I said, "is to try and recover his earliest musical influence. Sometimes that will short-circuit these episodes. But not always." I grabbed Argo's chin and held his head up against the wall. "Hey in there!" I shouted. "Take the last train to Clarksville! — And then what happens?"

"You're going to snap him out of it with a Monkees song?" Blake was incredulous.

"It's the first pop record he ever memorized," I said. "It's the foundation for all of his creative development." I looked back at Argo. His eyes seemed like they were trying to focus on me.

"And I'll meet you at the station!" he suddenly cried.

"What'll we have time for?" I demanded.

"We'll have time for coffee-flavored kisses. And a bit of conversation!" Recognition spread over his face. I slapped his cheek, and he looked around the room, puzzled and concerned.

"What's going on?" he asked.

"You are!" I said. "There's two thousand fans out in that auditorium, and you just had a little dizzy spell, but you're solid as a rock now."

"Well, for cryin' out loud!" he bellowed. "Let's not keep the crowd in suspense!" He rushed past me and bolted out the door. Freida was close behind him.

"There goes a true professional," I said. Blake let out a sigh of relief and slumped into a chair.

The room vibrated with a thunderous roar from the audience, and we heard the opening chords of Argo's guitar.

"Come on, Blake," I said. "The show is on. You've got a happy crowd and a hot band. The two best sounds in the world."

"It's mostly just noise," he said, lighting a cigarette. "And right now it's giving me a giant headache."

The Big Chill

The on-duty clerk, a skinny kid with a bad complexion, coughed and scratched his head as he looked at my papers. The badge on his white jacket said his name was 'Evan.' "Now, tell me again what this is all about," he said.

"I want you to re-activate my membership," I said, trying to speak clearly, so there'd be no misunderstanding. "Back when I joined this health club, they told me I could put my membership on hold if I went away on vacation. And it would stay on hold for as long as I was gone. So that's what I did. And now I'm back, and I want to re-activate my membership and start working out again."

Evan looked at my plastic identification card and then stared at the papers some more. "I dunno," he said. "Eight years is a long time."

"I can't help that," I said. "I was frozen in a glacier in Alaska. I'm lucky they found me at all."

"Frozen?" he said. "Hey, you're the Iceman, aren't you. I heard about you on the news."

"Please don't call me that," I said. "I really hate it. It sounds like I'm some kind of freak."

"We need to talk to Dan," the kid said. "He's out on the floor right now. I'm not authorized to do this stuff."

Dan came into the office shining with a nice fresh coat of sweat. He wore a towel around his neck, a blue tank top, and white tennis shorts. We shook hands tentatively, and Evan handed him the paperwork and tried to explain my request.

"Boy, I dunno," Dan said. "Problem is, the club has changed hands about four times since you signed up. See, you joined HealthMax. Then it got sold to PowerBodies. Then it was something else, and now we're Total Fitness."

"Janice said it wouldn't matter even if the club got sold," I answered. "She told me that explicitly."

"Who's Janice?" Evan asked.

"The salesperson who signed me up," I said. "She filled out the contract right in this office."

Another tanned, glassy-eyed adonis walked in right then. He was wearing a white jacket like Evan's, and his badge said 'Cory.'

"You ever know anybody working here named Janice?" Dan asked.

"Doesn't ring a bell," Cory answered. "What'd she look like?"

"Blonde," I said. "Long, straight hair. Five-foot-two."

"You look familiar," Cory said. "Say, are you that guy that got frozen? The Iceman?"

"Could you not make a big deal out of it?" I said, feeling a bit exasperated.

"So this is your original contract?" Dan asked, holding up one of the papers I had brought in.

"Yes," I said. "I kept it in a special fireproof lockbox at my house. With my social security card and my passport."

"How come you want to start working out again, anyway?" Evan wondered. "I mean, shoot, if I got frozen for eight years, I'd rather be out chasin' some tail. Make up for lost time."

"Well, for some reason that doesn't surprise me," I snapped. "Look, I was just out of college when the accident happened. I never got a job. My friends have all drifted away. I'm trying to re-build my whole life, and the only thing I have to start with now is my health club membership. I don't know why you people can't cut me some slack."

"The prices have gone way up since you joined," Dan said. "See, you're asking us to give you, for free, a service that costs our current members hundreds of dollars a year. We can't take too many hits like that, or our bottom line is dog meat!"

"We're not talking about a lot of deals," I protested. "We're just talking about one deal, and that deal is me."

"So, did you, like, fall into the glacier?" Cory asked. "Or were you buried in an avalanche?"

"I don't remember," I said, trying not to get angry. "I was out walking on the surface of the ice, and the next thing I remember is waking up in a hospital room."

"I thought all the glaciers melted a long time ago," Evan said. "Isn't that how the oceans got filled up?"

"The Mendenhall Glacier is still intact," I said.

"What'd they feed you in the hospital?" Cory asked. "You musta been awful hungry when you woke up. I get hungry just sleeping overnight." He lifted up his white jacket and t-shirt to reveal rippling washboard abdominal muscles. Then he slammed his fist into his midsection a couple of times, trying to impress me.

"Look," said Dan, "you bought a two-year membership, right?" I nodded. Cory tucked his t-shirt back into his pants. Evan was absent-mindedly picking at a pimple.

"Okay," Dan went on, "I could maybe give you a price break. How about a fifty-percent discount for the first year and twenty-five-percent for the second? That's the best I can do."

We haggled for awhile, and I finally got him to give me both years at half-price. And he told me that if I took a vacation or got hurt, there would be no extensions on the membership.

* * *

Later that afternoon, I was working out on a Stairmaster when a rangy, handsome guy stepped onto the machine next to me. We looked at each other, and there was something familiar about him.

"Excuse me," I said, "were you on TV lately?" He sighed.

"Yeah, on the news," he said. "I'm the guy who woke up from the coma last month."

"That's right!" I said. "You're the one they call the Sleeper! Unconscious for nine-and-a-half years!"

"Could you lower your voice?" he said. "I'm really getting tired of all the fuss."

"Hey, I know the feeling," I said. "I'm the Iceman. Does that ring a bell?"

"Oh sure," he said, "I didn't know you lived around here. Why'd you pick this club, anyway? The rates are pretty steep."

"Don't get me started on that," I said. "I actually signed up before my accident. Paid for two years up front. So today I find out they won't honor the agreement. They think I should be happy to get a discount on a new two-year deal. Jeez, I feel like the unluckiest person in the world."

"No way," said The Sleeper. "I joined up here and went into the coma after my second workout. But then my parents got into a nasty divorce, and there was a custody battle over who would take care of me, and all my personal files were lost.

"So when I came back last week to ask for an extension on my membership, there was no proof that I'd ever joined the club in the first place. The only deal they offered was three months for no charge, and a discount on vitamins. I'm definitely a whole lot unluckier than you are."

Neither of us noticed that Dan had come up behind the machines and was eavesdropping on our conversation.

"Hey," he said, "I've only been manager here for ten days, and I've already been hassled by two people involved in freak accidents who think they should get free passes for two years. But you don't hear *me* whining about being unlucky."

"Well, we're all in the same lousy boat," the Sleeper said. "Sometimes there's no way to catch a break in this stupid world."

I nodded. It didn't make me feel any better, but at least it was something we could all agree on.

Stay Happy

KENT: Okay, welcome back to *Good Morning Northwest.* Our time is seven fifty-two. I'm Kent Hollenbeck.

LISA: And I'm Lisa Sondergaard.

KENT: And if you're just joining us, the answer is *yes*, we *did* get smacked by something big about five hours ago. Not sure yet if it was an asteroid or a huge meteor, but it was a doozy! Serious damage reported in all major cities across the region, and millions of people are without electricity right now.

LISA: We've got the emergency generators running here at the station, and we know lots of you have TVs that run on batteries or other alternative energy sources. Hats off to good planning!

KENT: We're focusing on the immediate problems that most folks will have to deal with in the next few days, and our next guest is very well qualified to talk about this subject.

LISA: Dr. Samuel Goldendale is a psychologist and a lecturer who specializes in coping skills. Welcome, Dr. Goldendale.

DOC: Thank you. A pleasure to be here.

KENT: When we were chatting off the air, you mentioned that a person's attitude is very important under these conditions.

DOC: Right, Kent. There's a natural inclination to look around and say, 'Gee, the power is off, my house collapsed, the city is destroyed,' or what-have-you. And that's a very negative outlook.

LISA: And you say a better viewpoint is to see all this as an opportunity rather than a liability.

DOC: Exactly. For example, if you're searching for a missing pet, or a relative, get the neighbors to help out. One of the unfortunate trends of modern society is that a lot of people don't even know who lives next door. So use this chance to re-introduce yourself, and get that community spirit working again.

KENT: You were also pointing out that we have a lot to be grateful about, even in the aftermath of a disaster like this.

DOC: Right. Exactly. The typical response when you wake up and see all the damage is to say, 'Oh God, this is too much, I can't deal with it.' But the fact that you woke up at all is great news! It means you've survived the worst catastrophe of the century. And statistically, the chances of Earth getting hit by another celestial object in our lifetime are nil. Not gonna happen.

LISA: Okay, but suppose you've lost your home, lost your family perhaps, everything just wiped away. How do you get motivated?

DOC: One thing that I recommend is 'realistic re-evaluation.' Again, we want to create a plus out of a minus. Think about your spouse and family. Were you really getting along well? Did you honestly love the house? In many cases, the answer is no. So this kind of decisive change is actually beneficial in the long run. It allows you to basically start all over again with a clean slate.

KENT: Historically, you say that natural disasters have always created opportunities, and we just have to spot them.

DOC: Correct. When the plague swept across Europe in the Middle Ages, one of the results was a housing surplus in many areas. Lots of nice homes were sitting vacant, so working-class people started moving in and elevating their living standards overnight.

KENT: Same with jobs, too, I assume?

DOC: Oh yes. Exactly. Labor shortages mean better wages

for the surviving workers. I can almost guarantee that the next few years will be extremely important from an economic standpoint.

LISA: What I hear you saying is that we should consider every day as a kind of stepping stone.

DOC: Right, or building blocks in a foundation. We're building a whole new base of knowledge for everyday use, whether it's learning to identify edible plants to augment our diet, or different types of diseases like diphtheria and tetanus. All these things add up.

KENT: Since you mentioned disease, let's talk about the health issues. With so many streets and highways completely wrecked, folks will be doing a lot more walking, right?

DOC: Walking, bike riding, absolutely. And this additional exercise is a good thing, it improves your heart rate, gets rid of excess body fat—

LISA: Hey, there we go! Less fat!

DOC: You bet. One other thing to keep in mind is that the impact of this mystery object threw a lot of dust and other tiny particles into the atmosphere. That'll cut down on ultraviolet radiation, so if you don't have any clothing you can just go *naturel* and not worry too much about sunburn.

LISA: By the way, our fitness expert, Veronica Jensen, will be along in the next segment with some terrific tips for avoiding back strain. If you need to move pieces of wreckage or other awkward, heavy objects, she'll show you the right way to do it.

KENT: Lift with the legs, right?

LISA: I'll let you and Veronica work that out.

KENT: And her legs look way better than mine! Also, our household handyman, Bob Monroe, will explain what to do when you encounter broken electrical wires or ruptured gas lines.

LISA: And we have a brand new feature starting today. We call it 'Things To Do in the Dark.'

KENT: Until power is restored, a lot of people are going to feel pretty bored after the sun goes down. So if you have ideas for the nocturnally challenged, our phone number is 823-GMNW. We'll put the best suggestions on the air every Tuesday and Thursday.

LISA: And remember, if you have PacWest Soft-Touch cellular service, that's a free call.

KENT: Dr. Goldendale, thanks for joining us this morning. Terrific advice, and I know it gave our viewers a real boost.

DOC: Great to be here, Kent. I've always been a big fan.

LISA: Very quickly, Doctor, bottom line, the one thing we should keep telling ourselves day after day — Yes, there's been a major, life-changing disaster. But hey, it's not the end of the world!

DOC: Exactly.

Winner Take All

Thank goodness for youth soccer. By participating in this wonderful sport, our family has been transformed.

I had misgivings about having our daughter join the local team, no doubt about that. We've always been considered outsiders. My wife and I are both quiet, introspective, thoughtful people. So is our daughter.

But now we have a more spontaneous, outgoing attitude. Last Saturday was the final game of the season and the start of what I believe will be an exciting new chapter in our lives.

"Pearl!" the coach screamed at my girl. "Get the hell with it! Where is your brain?!"

"Calm yourself," I suggested. "She's only a second-grader." The coach, Mr. Crumley, looked at me with disdain.

"The goalie must pay attention to the action," he said, "even when the ball is at the other end of the field. Your kid is always staring up at the sky. It's a terrible habit, and she's done it for the whole blasted season!"

"Pearl has deep thoughts," I said. "Maybe she's thinking up a cure for cancer right now." It was an inspiring possibility.

"Oh yeah, that's how all the big scientific breakthroughs in history have come about," Coach Crumley said, contemptuously.

"Well, it does happen sometimes," I said. "Philo Farnsworth claimed that he invented television while working in a field as a teenager. Looking at the long rows of plowed furrows led him to believe that visual images could be transmitted across great distances by using horizontal lines of electrons."

Coach Crumley glared at me and then he shook his head. "Were you born weird, or do you work at it?" he growled.

"And not only that," interrupted Bagley Peterson, another parent who was standing nearby, "you're also dead wrong about Philo Farnsworth inventing television. It was the pioneering work of Vladimir Zworykin that really counted."

"Actually, that's the story the RCA people would like you to believe," I said. "Zworykin was their hired gun. But Farnsworth sued to protect his patents, and the courts eventually ruled in his favor. You can look it up if you want."

"I never even heard of Philo Farnsworth," snapped Carrie Stochausen, who always stayed away from me at the games. "If he was so great, how come no one's made a movie about him?"

"We're drifting off the subject," I said. "Perhaps my daughter is looking at the sky for answers to some kind of astronomical question. Just the other day, she was asking me to explain how the solar system was formed. We had a lively debate about whether or not Pluto is a true planet."

"Oh God, here it comes," chimed in Elliot Wentworth, one of the assistant coaches. "I suppose you're one of those skeptics who believe that Pluto is technically an asteroid. Well, it's not! It's round, it has an atmosphere, and it has a satellite."

"Charon," I said, nodding. Nobody responded. "Charon is the name of Pluto's satellite," I added.

"There you go again!" Carrie declared angrily. "You're always tossing out bits of arcane information with that little smug tone of superiority. And you wonder why you don't have any friends!"

"We're not stupid people," said Warren Spicak, who had wandered over as the discussion intensified. "This is a college town, with high-tech industries and a sophisticated workforce. We don't take kindly to newcomers who move in and try to undermine the intellectual self-esteem of our clannish, tightly-knit community. And it doesn't help that you're always wearing peculiar hats!"

"What's wrong with my hat?" I said, removing it from my head for a quick inspection. "It's your basic derby. Is that bad?"

"No, but it's damn strange," said Coach Crumley.

"Your wardrobe is oddly inappropriate," Elliot Wentworth said. "Green leisure suits and a brown derby. You look like Babar the elephant wandering the streets of Paris."

"We haven't done anything to warrant this overt hostility," said my wife, gripping my hand for moral support. By now, we were completely surrounded by scowling soccer moms and dads.

"Lady, you are a piece of work!" Elliot countered. "You're wearing a jeweled tiara at a kids' soccer match! Normal people don't do things like that."

"It's just a toy," my wife answered. "Pearl bought it for me at Toy Barn, and if I don't wear it she'll be disappointed."

"She's not gonna be on my team next year," Coach Crumley said. "The kid is in some other dimension most of the time. She never listens, and she gives my other players the heebie-jeebies."

"Hey," Warren said, "wasn't it sunny just a minute ago?"

I looked up and saw dark clouds boiling overhead. The kids on the field suddenly stopped chasing the ball. There was an eerie silence, and I noticed that Pearl was reaching toward the sky with both arms outstretched.

"She's a menace!" someone yelled.

And then the air seemed to explode. A roaring clap of thunder erupted over the field like a bomb, knocking every-one flat onto the brown grass.

When I sat up, Pearl was standing beside me, looking confused and embarrassed. "I'm sorry!" she said, trying not to cry. "I just wanted them to stop being mean!" Her lower lip quivered.

"I know, honey," I agreed, "I know exactly how you feel."

"And it's okay to feel that way," my wife added, pushing herself up onto her knees and staring at me with an apprehensive expression.

The others were scattered around us, all of them lying motionless where they had fallen. I reached down and picked up Carrie Stochausen. She was thirteen inches tall, with cloth skin.

"Have you turned people into dolls before?" I asked.

"No," Pearl said. "Just a dog. But I'll make them go back the way they were. It's not hard. I can do it, I promise!"

"Hold on!" I said. "Just relax. Let's take a quiet break."

"This is certainly an interesting development," my wife said.

"Very much so," I agreed. "And there's no need to rush into any decision right now. Let's load everybody into the car and discuss the situation at home."

* * *

Pearl is keeping our tiny guests in her toybox for the time being. All except for Coach Crumley, who is perched on my dresser. His little scowling face is almost endearing.

"I'm thinking about how nice it will be to have people show us a little more respect," I said to my wife that night as we reclined together in bed. "What are you thinking about?"

"So many dolls for just one girl," she answered. "Sometimes I worry about her being an only child. I don't want her to get spoiled and turn into a brat."

"Well, it's not too late to have another one," I said.

"I've thought about that," she replied. "The only risky part is that we might end up with a boy."

"Good point," I agreed. "Let's not push our luck."

Basic Instinct

Why do smart investors make dumb decisions? Because they are human beings — prisoners of passion who are bound to make irrational choices.

So say a bunch of behavior experts who gathered recently . . . at the Harvard Faculty Club.

"This is a biological problem; humans are not evolved for [active] investing," says Jay Pactel, professor of finance at Boston College.

—*The Wall Street Journal*, May 31, 1996

So this guy, this really angry-looking guy, just comes up to me on the street and shoves a leash in my hand. "Here," he says, "get this animal out of my sight!" And then he walks away, muttering and shaking his head, and I'm stuck holding a mutt that looks like a failed science project, sort of a collie/German shepherd mix that might also include genetic tissue from a sheep.

"Hey!" I yelled, but the guy was already out of sight.

"Let him go," said the dog. "He needs time to cool down."

I stared at the dog and then looked around to see if anyone else was listening. Turned out we were alone on that part of the sidewalk. "Did you really say that?" I asked.

"Yeah," said the dog. "Let's go somewhere quiet, like Forest Acres Park. I have a throbbing pain behind my ears."

I let him lead the way, and we ended up in a secluded corner of the park, away from car traffic and pedestrians. I sat on a rusting wrought-iron bench. The dog stretched out at my feet.

"Have you got a cigarette?" he asked.

"As a matter of fact, I do," I replied. "Camel Lights. I hope you don't mind the filter tip."

"I prefer the non-filtered, but it's okay," he said, raising his head up to give me a look of unconditional affection. I took the pack from my shirt pocket and slipped one of the smokes between his thin, canine lips. His eyes sparkled with delight when I snapped open my antique Zippo.

"You don't see those very often anymore," he said, taking a long drag.

"It belonged to my dad," I said. "Made it all the way through the Pacific Theater in World War Two."

"Glad to hear that," said the dog. "I suppose you're wondering why that other guy was so upset."

"I'm more intrigued by the fact that you have such highly developed communication skills," I replied.

"Yeah, well that's a separate issue," the dog said.

"So what's the story with your angry friend?"

"He's very mad because he just lost a lot of money for one of our clients," the dog said. "We work for Leeson Brothers, the biggest stock brokerage firm in town."

"We?"

"Yeah. His name's on the office door, but I'm the one who's supposed to track down the good deals. And I warned him not to get involved with anything in the restaurant sector right now, but he wouldn't listen. Did you hear about Burger Barn today?"

"I heard some big fast food chain filed for Chapter 11."

"That's the one. We're going to lose the client when he finds out that we've wrecked his portfolio, which is bad enough. But it also makes my partner look like a total idiot, since he disregarded my warnings. That kind of behavior is typical of your species."

"Let me see if I have this right," I said. "You, a dog, are giving investment advice to a stock broker?"

"Wake up and smell the flea collar, pal," the dog said, flipping his lower jaw to knock the ash from his cigarette. "I suppose you have the quaint idea that profitable decisions are made after long hours of careful research by really intelligent humans."

"Well, that's what the TV commercials imply," I said. "Dean Witter never shows any dogs running around the office."

"If manure were music," said the dog, "Dean Witter would be a brass band. But don't quote me on that." He took another long pull on the cigarette.

"So what is your system for picking the winners?" I inquired. "Do you just put your nose up to the wind and sniff?"

"Actually, that's not a bad guess," the dog said. "Annual meetings of stockholders are my specialty. I can smell fear in the air, the tone of a lie. I know when the officers are wrapping up bad news in ribbons, and I'm not fooled when a smooth-talking CEO gets up and makes a rosy forecast that can't possibly come true. Those are details that can bring in the big bucks."

Without warning, he suddenly jumped up and spun around in a circle. The look on his face was confused. Then he seemed to regain his composure.

"What was that for?" I asked. "Did you get a premonition? Are interest rates about to go up?"

"No," he said, "But I think there may have been a serious earthquake in Paraguay. When I start to dance like that, it's usually related to some geological phenomenon. Anyway, if you want to know about interest rates, you should consult a turtle.

They're better at tracking long-range movements in the lending markets."

"Is it widely known that animals have evolved better investment skills than people?" I wondered.

"It is on Wall Street, but they're not going to let you hay-seeds on the outside find out," he replied, and then he effort-lessly blew smoke out of his mouth and immediately sucked it back into his nose. French inhaling, it's called. I suppose he learned it from a poodle.

"In the final analysis," he went on, "it's not a very useful or satisfying way to spend your time. We learned that several hundred thousand years ago, when canines ruled the Earth."

I must have looked startled.

"Just kidding about that last part," he said impishly.

"Although I'm skeptical," I said, "is there any advice you might have for a casual, small-time investor like me?"

"You mean," he said, taking a last puff and dropping the cigarette butt on the ground, "you mean something more specific than buy low, sell high?"

"Right. Maybe just the name of a particular company."

"It's against all my better nature," he said, "but since you seem like a person who can control your irrational impulses and illogical passions, I'll say one word: Nordstrom."

"Really?" I said. "I've heard the merchandising industry is pretty flat these days."

He rolled his eyes. "See?" he said. "You people are evolutionary control freaks."

"Sorry," I said. "I guess we've spent too much time at the top end of the food chain. Would you like another smoke?"

"No thanks," he said, sniffing the air intently. "I think Mr. Happy is nearby. He must be looking for us."

Right then I saw the guy coming around a corner. He

looked more relaxed now, and he actually smiled and waved when he saw us. I stood up from the bench as he approached.

"Gosh, I really appreciate this," he said, reaching out to shake my hand. "I'm sorry that I was so abrupt with you earlier. That was totally uncalled for, but I've been under a lot of pressure lately. Please accept my sincere apology." When our hands separated, I saw that he had slipped me a $20 bill.

"I hope the dog wasn't a pest," he said, taking the leash. "Sometimes he just gets to be more trouble than I can put up with. For the sake of my personal standing in this community, may I ask that you not mention this incident to anyone?"

"No problem," I said. "What's his name?"

"Most of the time I just call him Bonehead," the man said. "That should tell you everything you need to know."

The two of them turned and walked away without another word. I kept track of the market for a few days, and Nordstrom's stock didn't do a thing. I'm glad I held on to my money. I'm beginning to think the dog made up the whole story.

Glad You're Not Here

A group of people watched from a distance as my rubber boat came ashore on the beach. They were milling around the battered, rusting fuselage of a large commercial passenger jet that was half buried in the sand.

A man broke away from the crowd and ran toward me.

"Have you come to rescue us?" he asked.

"Maybe," I answered. "I mean, it's up to you. In the old days, there wouldn't have been any choice. But times have changed. Who are you, anyway?"

"Hamilton Bellwood," the man said. "And that jet over there was operated by Argus Airlines."

"Great flaming mackerel!" I exclaimed. "You must be the survivors of Flight 1313! People are still debating what really happened to you folks."

"There was engine trouble," Hamilton said, "and the radio went dead, so we couldn't send out a mayday message. But the pilot made a perfect belly landing on this island, and nobody even got a scratch. Is that your ship way out beyond the coral reef?"

"Yes," I said. "It's sort of a floating university. We're surveying areas of the Pacific that haven't been fully mapped. This place isn't on any charts, so I volunteered to check it out."

"And I volunteered to come and meet you," Hamilton replied. "Many of the others are nervous about your intentions, so I told them to stay by the plane. Do you want to look around?"

"Oh, by all means," I said. "This is a fantastic achievement! To have sustained yourselves under these primitive conditions for, well, I don't have to tell you how long it's been."

"Actually, we lost track of all that," he said.

"You what?"

"Well, some people had calendars in their business planners, but those ran out after a few years. Besides, we've found it more emotionally satisfying to live each day as it comes along. As the old saying goes, there's no time like the present."

He turned, and we began walking toward the treeline at the edge of the beach.

"I'll be very interested to see what kind of system you devised for storing and distributing fresh water," I said. "That must have been one of your very first priorities."

"Not really," he answered. "We've always had plenty of water. It rains here every three days. Comes down in buckets. Keeps everybody feeling springtime fresh."

"You look healthy and well-nourished," I said. "Have you been growing a variety of crops to maintain a well-balanced diet?"

He shook his head. "No. We had a couple of passengers who knew about lawn care and orchids, but nobody had ever done any serious gardening."

"So what have you been living on?"

"We found an amazing plant," he said. "Kind of a flowering mushroom. Tastes great, and fulfills all our nutritional needs."

The well-worn path we were following through the overgrowth led to a clearing. The first thing I noticed was a circular arrangement of logs.

"What a fine, natural setting for group prayer," I said. "Your Sunday worship services must be inspiring."

Hamilton looked chagrined. "To be honest, most people on

Flight 1313 didn't have strong religious beliefs. But we do have a Jungian psychologist and two naturopathic healers. This spot is used for self-esteem classes, dream analysis, and sensitivity workshops. It's helped all of us maintain a sense of personal empowerment."

We walked farther along and came to a small steel ladder that was attached to a raised platform. When I stepped up onto the platform, I realized it was an outdoor stage. "Did you build this with parts scavenged from the jetliner?" I inquired.

"Yes," Hamilton said. "We have live entertainment here every day. As you may recall, our flight originated in Los Angeles. We've got four stand-up comedians, several actors, a drama coach, and a team of crazy disk jockeys."

"Gee, doesn't that get boring after awhile? Watching the same people doing their routines over and over?"

"Oh no," he said. "This is a very proactive group of people. We have a regular schedule of amateur talent shows that produce a wealth of new material. Our co-pilot won top honors most recently with an original one-man performance entitled 'The Wit and Wisdom of Fighting Bob La Follette.' If we were back home now, it would definitely get picked up by public television."

I stepped off the platform and walked over to a row of simple huts that were all made of dried grass and bamboo. "This doesn't look like adequate housing for everybody," I said.

"These aren't dwellings," Hamilton answered. "It's where we all get together for Saturday Market. There's a booth for arts and crafts, fortune telling, a floating poker game, stuff like that. I operate a trading card shop every other weekend."

"How can that possibly be a viable enterprise?"

"Just lucky, I guess," he said. "I found a suitcase washed up on the beach one day, packed with sports memorabilia. It

45

must've dropped overboard from some cruise ship. You'd be amazed at what the tide brings in."

"I don't really need to see anymore," I said abruptly. "This is all rather pathetic, in my opinion."

He looked surprised by my harsh tone. There was a crackle of breaking twigs along the trail, and I heard footsteps approaching. Three men emerged from the jungle and walked toward us.

"Sounds like we got here just in time," said the leader, a tall fellow with a red beard. "What's so pathetic, mister?"

"Pretty much the whole set-up," I said. "This had all the makings of a heroic tale of human courage. But you haven't devised any survival techniques in case the food or water gives out. There doesn't seem to be much leadership, social organization, or a plan for the future. You're all just sitting around talking about your inner feelings and wondering how to entertain each other."

"We have to play the game with the cards we were dealt!" Hamilton retorted. "Flight 1313 was a cross-section of American society in the late 1990s. Young, upwardly mobile professionals. It's not like the movies. We didn't have an eccentric rocket scientist onboard who could repair the plane with shoelaces and old chewing gum, and then fly everybody home."

"I'd say we've done all right under the circumstances," said a short, round guy with thick glasses. "At least we didn't regress into a primitive, savage lifestyle, like those English schoolkids in *Lord of the Flies*."

"Darn right!" said the bearded man. "You tell 'im, Piggy!"

"Okay, you've made your point," I conceded. "I guess I just wanted this to be more inspiring. Look, I'll level with you. Things aren't going too well back in the old U. S. of A. these days. There's been a terrible drought for almost nine years, and a mutant parasite has pulverized the corn and wheat farmers.

That's why I was hoping you had come up with some innovations in water conservation or food production. Do you think the special mushroom you've been eating could be raised commercially?"

"There's a major side effect I neglected to mention," Hamilton said. "It contains some mysterious ingredient that completely neutralizes your libido."

"Which is not necessarily a bad thing," added the round guy. "Once you remove the sexual tension from a personal relationship, it makes all the other aspects more enjoyable. I've learned that women are incredibly smart, and they have a great sense of humor!"

"Thanks, but no thanks," I said. "You keep the mushrooms."

"We certainly will," the bearded guy said sarcastically. "It doesn't sound like you're offering us any tickets to paradise. What else is screwed up back in the outside world?"

"There's a big swine flu epidemic raging on the east coast," I admitted. "A lot of germs have become immune to antibiotics."

"What about the social security system?" Hamilton asked.

"Gone," I said. "Flat broke."

"Say, did the Cubs ever win the World Series?" the round guy wanted to know. "I grew up in Chicago."

"They don't exist anymore," I answered. "The team got sold, moved to California, and became the Bakersfield Road Runners."

"No!" The round guy grimaced, gasped a couple of times, and began panting like some kind of rabid animal. "Damn you people!" he yelled, his eyes wide and malevolent behind the thick lenses. "Damn you all to Hell!" Then came the little fist.

My lower lip was still bleeding when I got back to the ship, and there was a painful bruise on my chin.

48

"My God, you look terrible!" said the captain as he reached over the rail and pulled me onto the deck. "I knew I shouldn't have let you go alone. These remote islands may seem peaceful, but they can be full of dangerous surprises."

"No danger here," I assured him. "I just got careless."

"What happened? Did you find anything interesting?"

"Somewhat interesting," I said. "Mostly disappointing. And, worst of all, I'd have to say that none of it was very surprising."

Rejuvenation

"So this is the first time you've ever been treated by an orthopractor?" Lonnie asked.

"Yes," I answered. "You came highly recommended. By my hair stylist."

"Ah, Regina," he smiled. "Glad to hear that. She's a doll. And you say you've been having lower back pain?"

"Correct. It can be really intense when I get up from a chair or after I've been driving. It's a throbbing pain." I was resting on a padded table in his office, staring up at the ceiling.

"Okay, relax," he said, grasping my head with both hands. "The key to this procedure, and all such therapy, is confidence. If you believe it's helping, you'll get positive results. Now I'm going to do a little manipulation here, so you may hear a cracking sound. But it should make you feel better."

And with that, he lifted my head slightly off the table and gave it a twist. There was an audible snap, quite loud.

"Wow!" I gasped. Then he let my head down, walked over to his desk, and took something out of a drawer.

"Please close your eyes and relax even more," he said.

I heard him come back to the table, and felt his hand slide under my right shoulder blade. He lifted up suddenly, and there was another snap. In fact, this time it was much, much louder, almost like a gunshot. Then he gripped my forehead and twisted my head again, and a third explosive sound erupted.

"That should do it," Lonnie said calmly.

"My goodness, is that normal?" I asked, turning my neck

from side to side to make sure it wasn't broken. "Hard to believe the human body can make so much noise and still hold together."

"Cracking is a good sign. Very loud cracks are the best, because they release a lot of tension. Do you feel better?"

"Yes, I do," I nodded. Then I noticed a strong odor in the room. "Hey," I said, "that smells like gunpowder. What're you holding in your other hand?"

One hand was hidden behind his back. In response to my question, he shrugged. "Why concern yourself with that idea?"

"Just show me what you've got."

He brought the other hand into view, and I was a bit taken aback to see that he was holding a starter's pistol, the kind used at track meets. A thin wisp of smoke was curling out the barrel.

"You fired a gun to enhance the sound of your treatment?" I said. "That seems a bit extreme, don't you think?"

"Not at all," he said. "Anything we can do to raise your level of confidence will help the end result. We must focus all of our thoughts on the healing process!"

Lonnie shoved the gun into the waistband of his pants and then gave me a startled look. "Oh dear!" he exclaimed, "there's something very worrisome behind your left ear."

"Really?" I said. He reached out, grabbed my head again, and slowly massaged around the ear. When his hands came back into my line of sight, I saw that he was holding a chicken egg.

"This could've caused serious trouble," he said. "Let's check it out for bad influences."

"An egg behind my ear?" I said, somewhat sarcastically. "Really now, isn't this getting a bit silly?"

Without saying anything, Lonnie cracked the egg on the edge of his desk and then opened the shell and dumped the contents into a small porcelain bowl. There was no yoke, and not even any liquid. "Very interesting," Lonnie said, examining the bowl. "Here's a little ball of hair, some teeth, a fingernail. This could have been your evil twin, who never fully developed inside the womb. Good thing we got him out of your system."

"An egg full of bad karma? That sounds like an old gypsy con game," I said.

"No, if this was a con game, I would've told you that all of your money is radiating negative energy. Then I would have made you wrap some cash up in a sheet and put it out in the forest so that the bad energy would be absorbed by nature's goodness.

"But I'm *not* a dishonest person! I'm just trying to get you oriented in a positive direction. You must visualize wellness."

"That sounds wonderful," I said, "But honestly, aren't you really just talking about the placebo effect?"

"Call it what you will," Lonnie answered. "My professional responsibility is to make sure you leave here feeling empowered with good health! If you phone me tomorrow for more therapy, I haven't done my job. But you also have to be open-minded. Don't dismiss a particular form of treatment just because it doesn't fit into our western-based scientific tradition."

"Okay, fine," I said. "But I still don't believe you pulled that egg out of my head."

"Forget the egg," he said. "Old news. Come over here." He led me to a corner of the room, where a blanket was draped over a piece of furniture. He flung the blanket aside, revealing a long coffin-like box that was covered with aluminum foil.

"Lie down in there," he commanded. I stepped into the container and stretched out, flat on my back. Then Lonnie unbuttoned my shirt, and ran his hands over my stomach.

"Relax again," he said, "and even if you don't fully agree with the efficacy of my actions, keep in mind that a good therapist uses all available weapons in the battle against disease and physical deterioration. Remember, when we're done here, I don't want to see you back in my office for a good long time!"

And with that, he cupped one hand over my navel and began probing with his other hand. It looked as if he was actually shoving his fingers directly into my abdominal cavity. Then a small stream of blood began oozing out from under the cupped hand.

"I'm in!" he said, and as I looked on squeamishly he began pulling some reddish, gooey fibers out from the bloody area. "Boy, this stuff is bad news!" he exclaimed. "Out, vile jelly!"

"Is this your version of psychic surgery?" I inquired. "Something you picked up in the Philippines? That stuff you're supposedly pulling out of me looks like fish entrails."

"My, your knowledge of the world is extensive," Lonnie said. "In fact, I did learn this technique during a visit to Manila. And who cares what's really in my hands? As long as I'm holding onto it now, it can't possibly harm you!"

"All right, I'm not going to argue," I said. "I'm rolling with the flow now, honest. What else have you got planned?"

"Oh, just stay where you are," Lonnie said, taking the sticky mess in his hands and tossing it into a waste basket. Then he grabbed a sponge from a sink and wiped my tummy clean.

"You're getting a hefty dose of something wonderful by just lying there," he said. "Do you know what this enclosure is?"

"I'm guessing it's an orgone box," I answered. "Are you a follower of Wilhelm Reich?"

"He had some intriguing theories," Lonnie said. "And no one's ever proven conclusively that orgone energy doesn't exist!"

He helped me out of the box and directed me to sit in a chair beside his desk. Before I could protest, he had rolled up one of the sleeves on my shirt and was preparing a hypodermic needle.

"This will give you one more line of defense against the maladies of the outside world," he said, rubbing my arm with an antiseptic cotton swab.

"What is it, a vitamin-B shot?"

"It *might* be something like that," he said, plunging the needle into my arm. "But let's suppose that I have trained a team of medical specialists and shrunk them down to microscopic size, and I am now injecting these tiny aquanauts into your bloodstream, where they will spend the next few days fighting bacteria and viruses that try to invade your inner territories."

"Are they riding in a tiny submarine, like the scientists in *Fantastic Voyage?*"

"No, too expensive. My team just has super hi-tech scuba equipment. And when they start to return to normal size, they'll make a beeline for your sinus cavities and simply walk out through your nose. It usually happens at night while you're sleeping, so you won't even hear them leave the house. They've all undergone Navy SEAL training, so they're very quiet."

"If true, that would be a tremendous asset to my natural immune system," I said, playing along.

"Exactly my point," Lonnie agreed, withdrawing the needle. "So we're done! Return to your home and concentrate on all the positive results that we have set in motion today. Healing doesn't happen overnight. Don't even think about calling me for at least thirty days. I don't want return visits! I want you to take charge of yourself!"

With a firm handshake and one final squeeze on the back of my neck, Lonnie sent me on my way. But while I was riding the elevator, it occurred to me that he never mentioned anything about how I would be billed for the services.

When I returned to his office, the door was locked. Also, a new sign was posted on the frosted glass panel, at eye level. The sign said Wah-Cheng Import-Exports, Inc. I knocked on the door, and nothing happened. I knocked again, and a woman answered. She had long black hair streaked with gray, and she was wearing a flowered dress, black horn-rimmed glasses, and vivid red lipstick that was slightly smeared.

"What happened to the orthopractor?" I said, puzzled.

"I don't know what you're talking about," said the woman in a low, sultry voice. "Anyway, what does a big, strong man like you need a therapist for? You look healthy as a horse!"

And then I realized that the woman was really Lonnie.

"I need to talk with the orthopractor," I said, feeling skittish. Something about the idea of cross-dressing always gives me the jim-jams.

"Oh dear!" said the 'woman.' "Your virility is too much for my normal inhibitions! I must have you right now, in this office! Enslave me with your passion!"

The red lips puckered and moved toward me, so I turned and ran for the stairs. And suddenly everything got *really* weird. Because when I reached the ground floor and ran outside, there was a woman standing by a car parked at the curb.

"Please, someone!" she yelled, "save my husband!" And then I saw a man's legs sticking out from under the car, so I dashed over.

"He was changing a tire and the jack slipped!" the woman exclaimed as I grabbed the front bumper and lifted.

"Pull him out!" I ordered, and she dragged the man up onto the sidewalk. "Good thing he's got a rather bird-like physique," I said. "If he was any heavier, you couldn't have lifted him."

"He's my dance instructor," the woman said. "Oh God, I hope his legs are all right. We were going to tango this afternoon!" I called for an ambulance and explained the situation, and the dispatcher said, "You lifted a *car* off someone? That's impossible." It was getting much too complicated, so I decided the best thing to do was hang up the phone and get back to my house, which I did as quickly as possible.

I still can't figure out if the guy under the car was real or just another one of Lonnie's set-ups. But I'm feeling better right now than I have in years. So I guess there's no point in quibbling about the details.

Teachable Moment

It was about 4:30 in the afternoon, my favorite time of day. The students had gone home, and the classroom was quiet. I was at my desk, writing a sample ransom note that I planned to use the following morning to kick off a discussion of home defense issues.

The peaceful interlude ended abrubtly when the classroom door was flung open, and the massive figure of Hasbro Watkins strode toward me. Dressed in his trademark buckskin jacket and floppy leather frontier hat, he was accompanied by his son, Philbert, one of my fourth-graders. The little fellow was still wearing the school uniform, a tan blazer with black slacks. A small bow tie was slightly askew, as usual.

"The boy didn't learn enough today," Hasbro said, gesturing toward his pudgy offspring. Philbert looked embarrassed.

"Excuse me?"

"I said he didn't learn enough," Hasbro repeated. "So I'm bringin' him back. I pay good money for this fancy-pants academy, and you claim to have a better product than the public school. So if this customer ain't satisfied, you got to make things right."

"Mr. Watkins, your thinking is unorthodox," I said, "but your point is absolutely valid. You enrolled Philbert in the Liberty School to provide him with a superior learning environment which emphasizes constitutional rights. So tell me, is there some specific shortcoming we can focus on right now?"

"Well, he don't know a blessed thing about sidearms yet," Hasbro complained. "I was told that would be a major part of the curriculum here."

"Quite true," I said, "but we usually start that training later in the year. However, I will be glad to show you my lesson plan, and I think that will reassure you that our school is not falling short of your expectations."

We walked over to a glass display case that was chained shut and secured with two heavy padlocks. After inserting the proper keys, I opened the case and carefully removed a 1911-style Colt .45 auto-loading pistol. The stainless steel finish gleamed even in the dull twilight of the late afternoon sun.

"The first thing the kids always ask is whether an automatic is more effective at close range than a revolver," I said, holding the weapon out for Hasbro to inspect. He grasped it firmly in his right hand, checking to make sure the safety was properly secured.

"And what do you tell 'em?" he asked, taking mock-aim at one of the light fixtures in the ceiling.

"Individual preference," I said without hesitation. "I like the auto-pistols myself. Easier to conceal because of their slender dimensions. And quicker to re-load in a combat scenario."

"Unless the clip jams," Hasbro replied, raising one eyebrow knowingly. "Then you can put your head between your legs and kiss your ol' buttinski goodbye."

"Jamming shouldn't occur if the weapon is effectively cared for when not in use," I countered. "We make sure all the kids know the life-threatening implications of poor handgun maintenance."

"So far, so good," Hasbro said, softening a bit. "I can't say as I like the stainless steel, though. I prefer a non-glare, black oxide finish. The reflection from this piece would give away your position to an aerial recon spotter in a heartbeat."

"Only if you're careless," I said, not giving an inch. "Anyone being hunted from the air should never be on the move when the sun is up. Night is a commando's best friend."

"Will you be giving equal time to revolvers?" Hasbro asked. "I happen to think they're more reliable."

"The students will get plenty of action on both," I assured him. "But I must say that, in my experience, medium- and large-frame revolvers give kids trouble with the trigger reach. And many of them have poorly designed grips that make it difficult to control recoil. But I'm getting ahead of myself."

We looked at Philbert, who happened to be jamming one finger into his right nostril.

"Knock that off!" Hasbro commanded. "You'll never get your finger on the trigger if it's stuck up your nose all the time!"

"Is there a particular weapon you prefer?" I asked. Encouraging parental participation in the learning process is a top priority at Liberty School.

"Pretty much anything by Smith & Wesson," he said.

"Smith & Wesson sucks!" Philbert blurted. Hasbro's face instantly flushed a bright red.

"Where did you learn to talk trash like that?" he demanded.

"Russel Traxler says it all the time," the boy replied, cowering under his father's withering gaze.

"Russel is one of the sixth-graders," I explained. "The older students get a bit cocky sometimes, after they've passed the Basic Threat Management course. Boys will be boys, you know."

"That better not happen again," Hasbro said firmly, and I noticed Philbert's lower lip quiver just slightly.

"How do you like the feel of that pistol?" I asked, trying to ease the tension.

"Not bad," Hasbro answered. "Is it something special?"

"I covered the grip with a suede-like material, which gives me a better purchase on the weapon when my hands are sweaty."

"Very interesting," Hasbro nodded. "Although sweating is a good way to measure your own level of fear. I've learned to control my sweating, so I don't need a special grip."

"That's admirable," I said, trying not to sound cloying.

"In fact," Hasbro continued, "I have good command over all of my physical functions. I can suspend the elimination of bodily waste for a week if I feel like it! Anyone tracking me in open country is gonna have one hell of a hard time, by God. That's the kind of thing the schools oughta be teaching."

"I have to go to the bathroom!" Philbert suddenly squealed in a high-pitched voice, and before we could answer he had raced out of the classroom. Hasbro was thoroughly chagrined.

"The wife coddles him too damn much, in my opinion," he said. "How's a person gonna survive the danger and hostilities of this angry world when he can't even control his bladder?"

"Philbert works hard in class," I said, trying to be supportive. "But he does seem to lack self-confidence. Perhaps that will improve once he starts using live ammunition."

"And when does that happen?"

"The fourth-graders will begin on the practice range with static targets in the spring. Fifth grade is when we get into the draw-and-fire techniques. Sixth graders are into obscured-vision drills, multiple assailants, and rapid reloading."

"Well, sir," Hasbro said, handing me the pistol, "you seem to know your business, and I thank you for your time. I feel much better than I did when I came in here."

We shook hands, but he didn't seem completely satisfied.

"I have one more request," he said. "Some of the other parents have mentioned this to me also. It would be nice if you could give the kids a few words of wisdom each day, so when they come home we have something to talk about. Do you get my drift?"

"I think so," I said. "How's this: When a man with some gold meets a man with a gun, it's easy to see who's going to end up with the gold and the gun."

"That's ex-*act*-ly what I mean!" he exclaimed.

Then the door swung open again, and young Philbert presented himself in a state of near-hysteria. Tears were streaming down his face, and I could see at once that his clothes were askew.

"Some older kids stole my pants!" he wailed. "And they tried to put my head in the potty, and they were laughing about it!" His gasping voice sounded like the braying of a wounded mule.

"Someone got the drop on you?" Hasbro said with a tone of disbelief and disgrace. "Son of a sea cook! I'm not gonna stand still for this!" He looked at me with a how-could-you-let-this-happen expression.

"A few of the sixth-grade boys have formed a secret club, and are pulling pranks after school," I said. "We're trying to squelch their activities without being overly authoritarian. Fortunately, I have some junior-size denim jeans in my desk drawer. Philbert can borrow them overnight."

"That's right neighborly of you," Hasbro said.

"This will be a good first lesson," I said. "Philbert, listen up. Wherever you go in life, speak softly, keep your powder dry, and make sure you have access to an extra pair of pants."

"Did Thomas Jefferson write that?" the boy asked.

"If he had lived long enough, he would have," I answered.

"Let's go, son," Hasbro said, motioning toward the door. Then he leaned close to me and said, "Because of you, I might

try and have a few more children, just so I can send them to
school here."

It was getting dark as they walked out the door. I was tired
but exhilarated, and carefully re-locked the gun rack. Then, satisfied that all was secure, I sat down at my desk, took out my
daily evaluation file, and gave myself a nice gold star.

Miranda 2000

You are under arrest. You have the right to remain silent. If you give up this right, anything you say can and will be used against you in a court of law. Plus, if you have a really juicy story, you could lose out big time in the long haul when everyone wants a piece of your action.

You have the right to speak to an attorney before questioning. If you wish to speak to an attorney and cannot afford one, an attorney will be provided for you. Be sure to check the message center when you get to the police station. News travels fast these days, and lawyers may already be lining up on your behalf.

You have the right to an agent. A good one will take immediate steps to protect all the subsidiary rights to your story, especially the book and movie rights, and foreign distribution.

You have the right to speak to the local media at some point, but make sure your lawyer and your agent are in the loop. The media has the right to do almost anything they want with your sound bites, so be careful what you give them.

You should have the right to script approval for TV or movie productions, but your lawyer will have to nail that down later.

Ditto for the right to approve which actor will play your role and whether or not you'll be allowed on the set during filming.

You have the right to set up a toll-free 800 number as soon as possible after being booked into custody. The phone company will handle the arrangements for this. Call the customer information line and ask for Maevis.

You have the right to a healthy diet while awaiting trial. If the standard jail fare is unacceptable, you will allowed to request alternative food items that are appropriate to your current lifestyle and caloric requirements.

You have the right to receive mail and to correspond with anyone who is interested in your case. If you receive photos of attractive pen pals and would like to arrange personal visits, you might consider contacting *Hard Copy* or *American Journal* so they can broadcast the proceedings.

You have the right to appear on *Larry King Live* at least four times per year, and Mr. King's producer will probably give you the right to submit your own questions ahead of time.

You have the right to a polling service so that you may stay informed about current public opinions regarding your case.

You will not be questioned further until you signify that you understand these rights and agree to move the process forward.

We're not trying to rush you into anything, but don't drag this out too long. The public has a short attention span. And if they get bored with your case, all the rights in the world aren't going to put you back in the limelight.

Now, shall we get down to business?

Mystery Achievement

There was a bright light up ahead, and I was slowly walking toward it. It seemed like I was in a long tunnel. Everything was dark and quiet, and so peaceful. I didn't feel any fear. I just kept moving toward the glow.

"Ooooooo—migosh!" said a juvenile female voice. I turned around and saw my pre-teen daughter standing behind me.

"Dad, are we like, you know, *dead*? This is *totally* creepy."

"Melanie, what are you doing here?" I asked.

"I was with you," she answered. "Don't you remember?"

"No, I don't." I looked toward the brightness again. "I feel like this is the way to go."

"Hello, Earth to Dad?" Boy was she saucy. "That's the *light*! That's what everybody sees when they croak. I just read a big article about it in *Rolling Stone*."

"I don't think we're dead," I insisted. "Come on."

We kept walking, and soon I could see the outline of a small stucco house. We approached the main window and looked into the living room. The brightness was coming from a TV set. But there was no picture on the screen, just fuzzy static.

A man was dozing in an easy chair. I tapped on the glass and woke him up. He squinted at us, slowly raised himself to a standing position, and walked toward the window. He appeared to wearing some kind of aviator's uniform.

"Oh, wow!" Mel exclaimed. "It's Wolfman Jack!"

"No way," I said. "It looks more like Caesar Romero with a goatee. But I don't understand the flight suit. Very weird."

The man reached down, removed his shoes, and pulled off his white socks. Then he carefully inserted his hands into the socks and began to perform a kind of puppet show.

"I think he's symbolically asking us to come inside," I said.

"Dad, if we go in there, we are *goners*!" Mel said. "I'm telling you — let's turn around *right now*."

Instead, I walked over to the front door. It was completely covered over with bumper stickers. They were all identical, with a picture of a toilet on the left side and the words 'Hush, Don't Flush' on the right side.

"That makes no sense at all," Melanie said.

"Wait a minute," I said. "I was looking at toilets the other day, at that plumbing supply store. We need to get a new one for the downstairs bathroom, remember?"

She looked at me with her patented how-can-someone-as-odd-as-you-be-my-real-father? expression.

"Don't you see?" I said. "This is simply a dream. All these crazy details are coming out of my subconscious mind."

"So, you're saying I'm just a detail? Or are we *both* having the *same* dream at the *same* time?"

"You do have a point there," I admitted. "However, dream or no dream, I'm going inside."

The door swung open easily. There was mail all over the floor, thousands of envelopes in all shapes and sizes. Melanie picked one up. The envelope had the word 'Yes' written in the upper right hand corner where a stamp normally goes. And the word 'Return' was written in the lower left hand corner.

"They're all like that," Mel said. "This is bizarro!"

"Maybe it's some kind of experiment," I said. "Could we be wired up to, like, a machine that causes hallucinations? If we were wired together, that would explain why we're both seeing the same things here."

"Dad," Mel said, shaking her head, "that sounds like the plot of a really dumb movie. James Brolin would be starring in it." At that moment the man wearing the socks on his hands walked past us and disappeared out the front door.

"Hey!" I yelled, but he seemed not to hear me.

"That is the ghost of Wolfman Jack! Sweartagod!" Mel said.

"Let me ask you something," I said. "If that guy really was a ghost, why did he have clothes on?"

"Excuse me? Am I a fashion expert for dead people?"

"Well, think about it," I said. "Ghosts are supposed to be spirits. Why should spirits need to wear anything? When you die, your clothes don't go with you into the spirit world. That's why I'm sure we're not dead right now. Come on, let's look around."

I walked into the living room, where the TV was still generating only white noise. I reached down to turn it off, but there were no knobs or control buttons. I found where it was plugged into a wall outlet and yanked out the cord, but the set would not turn off.

"Cable trouble in the afterlife," Mel said. "This room is really skanky. I wonder how come it doesn't smell bad?"

"That is an excellent question," I said, sniffing the air. "It doesn't smell like anything. I'd say it's more evidence that we're in a dream. Let's see what else is here."

There was a hallway leading toward the back of the house. I proceeded down the hall a few feet, until I came to a door that was slightly open. I could see the edge of a bed inside the room.

"Dad! Omigosh!"

"Now what?" I said grumpily. "Really, Melanie, you have an attitude problem. It's getting tiresome."

"Dad, I would *not* go in there," she said. "This is just like *2001: A Space Odyssey*, toward the end, where the astronaut sees himself lying in the bed, and he's an old man. And then he turns into the big baby floating in outer space, remember? This must be some kind of time-warp deal. I bet aliens are watching us!"

Her story sounded so plausible that I got a little spooked. Instead of just walking into the room, I gave the door a hard push and stood cautiously in the hall. The bed was empty.

"So much for the time warp," I said.

Just then we heard a crashing sound from the front of the house, and the walls of the room shuddered. A flood of greenish-colored water began pouring through the bedroom door, and I was swept off my feet. When my head re-surfaced, I realized the water was floating me toward the ceiling, except the ceiling was gone and I saw patches of blue sky and thick clouds overhead.

A hand was reaching out to me. I grabbed it and felt myself pulled out of the water, gasping as I fell into a long, inflatable rubber raft. My vision was blurred, and I had to blink several times before the world came back into focus. My wife was staring down at me with a frantic expression. Her hair and clothes were soaked, and the boat was bobbing up and down. Two swarthy-looking men were tending the outboard motor in the back end of the craft.

"What happened?" I said, coughing up briny-tasting water.

"You got swept overboard!" she answered. "We were out on the balcony of our cabin, and a gale came out of nowhere. Somebody said we were passing through a corner of the Bermuda Triangle! Planes have vanished here! I thought you were gone for good!"

"Santa Maria!" one of the men exclaimed, and both quickly made the sign of the cross.

"There was a little fountain of sparks around this spot, right before you popped up," she said. "It was like a sign." She looked at the two men. "Back to the ship, amigos! Pronto, pronto!"

She began waving. I looked over the edge of the raft and saw a luxury cruise liner a short distance away.

"Wait!" I yelled. "What about Melanie?"

"Who?"

"Our daughter!" I said. "Where is she?"

"She isn't due for three months," my wife answered, pointing toward her rotund mid-section. "That's why we took this cruise, don't you remember? It's our last vacation before parenthood."

The crewmen got the motor started, and we turned back toward the ship. A light drizzle started falling.

"Melanie is a actually a very pretty name," my wife continued, thoughtfully. "I like it. Sounds a bit feisty, but smart."

"Yes," I said. "She's a handful. I mean, she *will* be."

Live At Five

"I'm Norman Conrad," said the news director, squeezing my hand so hard I thought I would hear bones snapping. "You must be Seth Applebee, the guy who thinks he can be a producer on my team."

"I don't think it, I *know* it," I said, batting his attitude right back in his face. "This newscast was made for me!" Norman's eyes danced, so I knew it was the correct approach.

"Sit over there," he said, pointing to a seat in a corner of the control booth. "And get your news glands pumped up."

"Ten seconds to airtime!" yelled Bryce, the director, a stocky twenty-something who sported a blond mohawk haircut. "Camera three, give me that two-shot of the anchors a little tighter!" he yelled into his headset. The atmosphere in the booth was crackling with nervous energy.

The male-female anchor team had fire in their eyes. The studio lights came up on cue, and the announcer's voice boomed out the introduction: "Now, coming to you as it happens, using all the resources of the Channel 4 newsroom, with Tux Redford and Plush Bennington. We don't just cover the news—WE MAKE OUR OWN! This is FAB-4 Action Livecast!"

"Are women who take self-defense classes really learning self-defense, or self-delusion?!" Plush exclaimed with breathless urgency. "We're going to find out right now, from our consumer expert, Marina Salgado, who's walking near Pier 37 down at the waterfront, one of the most crime-infested areas of the city."

"Push Marina full frame!" Bryce snapped, and there she was,

a lynx-like crusader for social justice, wearing a black trenchcoat with her waist-length hair tossing in the breeze.

"Plush," she began, "as you know, I just completed a popular new training technique called Never Fear Again, which is supposed to empower women with self-defense skills so that — OWWW!"

The picture on the monitor shuddered and went slightly out of focus, but we could see that someone had jumped in from the left side and was wrestling Marina to the ground. The assailant was a stringy-haired punk wearing a denim jacket and black army boots.

"Marina!" Tux said urgently, "tell us what's happening!"

"Let me go—! Jerk!" The transmission was garbling badly. We could hear grunting, and angry scuffling sounds.

"Hey, kid," Norman called to me. "What would you do now?"

"Leave Marina up for a few more seconds," I suggested. "Get the viewers tantilized before you cut away."

"I'm starting to like you, kid," Norman said. Bryce, as if responding to my instructions, waited for exactly five more seconds and said to the anchors, "Okay, move it along!"

"We'll come back to that story in a moment," said Plush, "and find out out if Marina's No More Fear training really worked. But now, let's go to Larry Boyd on the eastside entrance ramp of the Gateway Narrows Bridge for a special FAB-4 citizen alert!"

"Thanks Plush," said Larry, and as the camera pulled back we could see cars jammed up in both directions behind him. "Suppose a terrorist gang tried to seize control of this bridge during rush hour? It's as easy as blocking off the exit lanes on each end with orange cones, which is exactly what our crew did a few minutes ago.

"Now these motorists are helpless! We could be raking their vehicles with machine-gun fire, inflicting terrible carnage. We asked city officials to comment on this horrendous but very real possibility earlier today. However, they didn't seem the least bit interested. I wonder how some of these drivers feel about putting their lives on the line out here? You sir, in the red Porsche. . ."

There was a growing blare of horns honking angrily in the background as Larry approached the Porsche. It was a convertible with the top down. The two yuppie-ish studs riding in it seemed bemused by all the commotion.

"Are you outraged that the city allows this bridge to operate with so little security in place?" Larry said, holding the microphone out toward the driver.

"Damn right!" the man said, with just the right balance of indignation and enthusiasm. "Those bureaucrats don't care about us little guys! We should clean out city hall!"

"Well, there you have it," Larry said. "Another serious problem that our politicians want to ignore, but we won't let them! Hey guys, what's your favorite news station?"

"FAB-4 Livecast!!" the Porsche duo shouted in unison. Then the driver reached out, grabbed Larry's microphone, and blurted, "Yo! Plush! I want to sex you up!"

In the studio, the anchors didn't miss a beat.

"Thanks, Larry," Tux said with a sly grin, "you be sure and tell that guy the line forms behind me!"

"Oh stop!" Plush giggled, touching Tux lightly on the arm. "You're terrible!"

Norman jumped out of his chair and punched the air. "Yes!" he cried. "Smutty innuendo in the first segment! There *is* a God!"

"I knew you'd get religion sooner or later," Bryce quipped.

It was a good time to lower the intensity of the show, so

Norman ordered an aerial view from SKY-4, the news chopper, with 'Top Gun' Ace Perry at the controls.

"What a fantastic day to be airborne!" he crooned. "Crystal clear skies in all directions, and right below me you can see the FAB-4 Prize Van driving northbound on the Forest Park Expressway."

The camera zoomed in on the white Dodge van as it cruised along at a leisurely pace.

"Some needy person in our audience will be receiving a surprise gift later in the show, so stay right here on FAB-4. And if you know someone who could use a helping hand, give us a call, and the prize van could be stopping at their door very soon!"

The pacing was perfect. I felt like I was dancing to the music of the spheres. After a commercial break, we jumped right into a compelling story at the Tri-County General Hospital.

"Tux and Plush," said Maynard Ogilvy, the medical specialist, "I'm here in surgical ward 3, undergoing a complete replacement of both knee joints, which were damaged by years of improper jogging. It's also an exclusive look at a brand new procedure developed by Dr. Warren Edwards. How are things going so far, Doctor?"

"Maynard," said Dr. Edwards, "you'll be 'Sweatin'' to the Oldies' with Richard Simmons by this time next week! Let's show the folks at home what I've done here . . ."

I admit it was a bit startling, seeing bloody tissue and shiny surgical instruments in vivid, up-close detail, but I couldn't look away. Then a phone line in the booth started lighting up. Norman punched the call onto a speaker box, so we could all hear it.

"Some viewer wants to talk to you immediately," said a secretary. Norman motioned for me to come over and stand by his shoulder. There was a click on the speaker box, and then an elderly-sounding woman said, "How can you justify showing these awful pictures right at the dinner hour?"

I could feel everyone staring at me. This was obviously a major test of my abilities to fit into the FAB-4 system. "It's really quite simple, ma'am," I replied calmly. "This is news you can use." There was a pause.

"Oh," said the woman. "In that case, I guess it's all right."

"Thanks for making FAB-4 number one," I answered. As I returned to my seat, Norman gave me a crisp military salute.

Bryce cut back to Marina Salgado at Pier 37, who was sporting a small bruise under her right eye. The denim-clad attacker was now sitting cross-legged on the sidewalk with his hands cuffed behind his back. A burly police sergeant stood guard.

"Tux and Plush," Marina said, "I did have some doubts about the Never Fear Again training, but not anymore! With just a few simple moves, I was able to overpower an assailant who outweighs me by fifty pounds. He's now under arrest, but I want you all to know he's not some anonymous, inhuman predator. His name is Randall Grimes, and his story could be any child's story. Randy, tell me why you're out here tonite." She leaned down and put her hand on the kid's shoulder while he talked.

"Can't be worse on the street than back home," Randy said, sounding forlorn. "My dad's gonna pound me when he sobers up enough."

"You'll hear all of Randall's heartbreaking secrets next week," Marina said, "when you tune in for my five-part series, 'Throwaway Kids—The Dangerous Years.' Only on FAB-4 News!"

"Switch to Davey in the big fish tank!" Bryce commanded, and instantly we were seeing outdoor reporter Dave Leland submerged in full scuba gear. He was covering a wacky underwater wedding at SeaLand Aquarium.

The secretary buzzed again on the speaker box. "It's your favorite competitor," she said. "Martin Slansky, news director at Channel 8." I started to get up, but Norman looked over and gave me the 'stay put' sign with his palm.

"Put him through," he told the secretary.

"Hello, you walking pus-bag," Martin Slansky said with mock cheerfulness. "Another great harvest of stories from the gutter again tonite. Are you proud to be airing this crap?"

"Marty, old pal," Norman said, soothingly. "You're just getting cranky from spending so much time at the bottom of the ratings barrel. Is it dark down there?"

"Listen, slime-bucket," Martin replied, dropping all pretense of civility. "I'm gonna put a hefty dent in your numbers tonight. We have a nice little political scoop coming up. Watch your monitors. In about two minutes, Channel 8 will make headlines. Too bad your sources inside the city manager's office can't walk and chew gum."

"Sounds intriguing, booby," Norman said. "I suppose your hotshot investigator, Les Kentfield, is bringing home the bacon."

"Maybe," said Martin, sounding a bit suspicious. "How did you know Les was in on this thing?"

"When it comes to the news biz, I have a sixth *and* a seventh sense, booby," Norman chided. "For example, I'm aware you did *not* re-sign Les and his favorite cameraman when their contracts ran out two days ago. The word on the street is that you've put a freeze on all salaries after that last ratings disaster. Oh, there's Les right now, I see him on the monitor, just like you said."

Except it was the monitor for *our* show. "And now," said Plush, "let's welcome the newest member of the FAB-4 news team, political analyst Les Kentfield, who's about to expose a major scandal involving the city manager and some teenage call girls."

"Plush, it's a story so shocking I'm almost ashamed to report it," Les said, grimacing. "And it's happening in the office right behind me, the office of a man who says he's happily married. Let's step through this door and get a FAB-4 exclusive look at what our tax money is paying for."

It all bloomed on-camera like a savage rose: the city manager in his Jockey shorts, the girls running for cover, and on the speaker box we heard the almost inhuman curses of Martin Slansky through the telephone line. "SATAN!" he screamed. "Monster! You bloodless, rat-eating animal! I'll see you in hell for this!"

Bryce grinned hugely during the tirade. "Awesome," he said to Norman. "Hiring your competition's top reporter on the air—I'm truly impressed."

The last part of the show was a glide. Dave Leland broke up the underwater wedding by writing a message to the bride revealing that her groom was already married to another woman. The scene was quickly obscured by a hurricane of air bubbles as the guests began pummeling the hapless bigamist.

"You know," I said, deciding it was time for an unsolicited opinion, "it would have been *really* good if Dave had actually brought along that other wife to the ceremony. Then she could have gotten into the action, right?" Norman rubbed his chin thoughtfully, and then nodded.

"I like your style, kid," he said with a sly tone.

Then the FAB-4 Prize Van made a heartwarming stop at the home of Elbert and Louise Fluggel, and the crew presented the elderly couple with a brand new Kenmore washer and dryer. Just a few days previously, we learned, the Fluggels had lost most of their major appliances to a ring of con artists posing as traveling repairmen.

"Oh, you wonderful people," Louise blubbered as tears streamed down her cheeks. "I believe in miracles, I surely do!"

"God must be watching over us!" Elbert chimed in.

"Mr. Fluggel, I certainly hope so," Plush replied in the studio, "because that means he's watching FAB-4 News right now!"

"Amen to that!" Tux added.

Bryce wrapped it all up by cutting to a split-screen view with the Fluggels on the right side and a live shot of Maynard Ogilvy on the left, standing up on his brand new knee joints and waving jubilantly from the recovery room.

"Roll credits!" Bryce yelled, and then he turned and fixed me with a blazing stare. He looked like a horse that had been ridden hard and put away wet. "What a show!" he exclaimed. "Hey you, Seth-man! Where the hell are you ever gonna see a better news program than the one we just did?!" It was clearly a challenge.

"I'll tell you where!" I yelled back instantly, pounding my fist on the desk for emphasis. "Listen up, everybody. There's gonna be a better news show, and I'm gonna produce it, and it's gonna be right here! In our studio! Same time! TOMORROW NIGHT!!" And that's exactly what happened.

We Can Work It Out

I knew that my beeper was about to go off. It's a talent I have developed over the years. My occupation requires an elevated level of sensitivity to all forms of communication.

The address displayed was a familiar one. I've been there many times. For a moment, I felt a twinge of frustration. But I, Karliss, Master of Successful Negotiation, have never shied away from a difficult case. My workshops have been attended by thousands of citizens from all walks of life, and for an extra fee I offer a special 800 number for emergency in-home assistance.

Within seconds, my car was roaring toward the troubled residence of Lyle and Jarellen Killingsworth. The front door was unlocked, and my intuition told me to head for the kitchen.

The strong-willed couple was standing in front of the sink, face to face, just a few inches apart, glaring at each other like two fighters at the start of a boxing match.

"Wait!" I said, holding up my hand. "You are now posturing, which is absolutely non-productive. Successful negotiation requires room to maneuver, both physically and intellectually. Each of you take a step backward. That will reduce the level of tension and create space for me to enter into the process."

"I'm concerned that stepping back might be interpreted as a sign of weakness," Lyle said, never looking away from Jarellen.

"Not necessarily," I said. "Remember Rule 17? Maximize potential avenues across disputed territory. You can't negotiate when you're eyeball-to-eyeball. My seminar explained twelve ways to avoid creating an impasse, which you have obviously ignored."

I waited, but neither of them even blinked.

"I'm counting to three," I said, "and then I move up to the sink. One, two, three!" They stepped apart, although Lyle waited just a fraction of a second, so that Jarellen went first.

"There is a coffee cup in the sink," I observed. "Is this the focus of your current disagreement?"

"Yes," Jarellen said. "He wanted a cappuccino after dinner. So I made it for him. And served it in that cup."

"You made a latte, not a cappuccino," Lyle snapped.

"It was a cap," she replied. "But he wanted extra foam."

"If it doesn't have enough foam, it is *not* a cappuccino!"

"All right," I said, "we've established a starting point. What happened to the beverage?"

"I drank it," Lyle said through clenched teeth. "I opted for conciliation. But then she refused to take the cup away."

"I was cleaning the espresso machine!" Jarellen said. "Bear in mind that I prepared a nice dinner, cleared the table, loaded the dishwasher, got his coffee, and it seemed reasonable that he could offer some assistance."

"The dinner was bland," he responded, "and she used our good china, which is supposed to be reserved for guests. I avoided a whole series of potential conflicts throughout the meal. And then she has the nerve to accuse me of being unreasonable!"

"So how did the cup get in here?" I asked.

"I caved in," he said. "She creates a 'good guy/bad guy' scenario and manipulates it brilliantly at my expense."

"All I want is one complete gesture of cooperation!" she shot back. "He brings the cup all the way to the sink, rinses it, and sets it under the faucet. As if he can't take one more second out of his busy schedule to stick it in the dishwasher! So here we are. Someone other than *me* is going to wash that cup."

"I don't deserve this at all," Lyle said, sighing loudly.

"A successful person doesn't get what he deserves," I pointed out. "He gets what he negotiates. But you can't hit the target when it's constantly moving around. That's Rule 23. Are you people listening to my Karliss audio tapes on a regular basis?"

"We haven't been able to agree on a schedule for that," Jarellen confessed. "And every time I bring it up, he accuses me of trying to impose a pre-arranged decision."

"That's a secondary issue," Lyle said. "We need to resolve the cup situation. Rule 29 says to stick with the game plan."

"Absolutely right," I agreed. "Although I do want to caution you both about this tendency to become deadlocked over elements of your life that some observers might consider trivial."

"If I'm not mistaken, Dr. Karliss," Lyle said acidly, "we are paying a significant sum for your professional services. Are you implying that your skills are improperly utilized here?"

"Not at all," I said. "The purpose of the Karliss system is to negotiate better deals for both parties, regardless of your economic status. My techniques have saved big corporations millions of dollars. But I know the roadblocks to a successful life come in all sizes."

"The cup is not trivial!" Lyle exclaimed. "I have spent the entire evening making one concession after another, with nothing to show for it!"

"You sat at the table like a lump while I did all the work!" Jarellen said, her eyes blazing.

"You should be glad that I didn't stand up and fling that wretched supper off the table," Lyle sniffed. "It took tremendous restraint on my part. And I know that I'm diminishing my character with each successive act of capitulation."

"Don't lower your expectations," I warned. "Rule 13 comes into play here. If you expect less, you'll get less."

"Exactly my point," Jarellen interjected. "My expectation is that someone who uses a coffee cup can put it in the dishwasher."

"The negative energy in this room is palpable," I said. "Perhaps we should take a recess and practice some resentment reduction techniques. Or, at the very least, change the pace of the negotiations."

"I've had the flu, and I don't want fatigue to become a factor," Lyle said. "On your previous visit, I believe she played to my weakness in that area."

"Not likely," Jarellen said, "since I ended up compromising on every point of contention."

"Refresh my memory," I said. "Are you referring to the disagreement over a certain kind of facial cleanser?"

"Yes," she said. "I asked him to buy me a tube of Apricot Scrubble. 'Scrubble' is a brand name. He brought home some cheap imitation, and refused to admit he had made a mistake."

"Because it was *not* a mistake. The label said 'apricot scrub with soothing elderflower.' The salesgirl assured me it was virtually an identical product." Lyle's tone was coolly adamant.

"Except you weren't buying it for the salesgirl," Jarellen pointed out. "I like Scrubble because it's more abrasive, and leaves my skin taut and tingling."

"Well, you are certainly becoming an expert spokes-person on abrasiveness," Lyle countered.

"We resolved that dispute by understanding how expectations go up and down even while negotiations are proceeding," I said. "As for the fatigue factor, keep Rule 33 in mind. You are stronger than you think."

I paused, and my instincts told me it was time for me to seize the moment with a decisive act. I reached into the sink and grabbed the cup. They were taken aback, as I anticipated.

"This is coming off the table, figuratively speaking," I said. "But rest assured, we are not walking away from the deal. I just think a cooling-off period would be useful to the process."

"What is the time frame you have in mind?" Lyle asked.

"Let's set a target of three days," I said. "Focus all of your skills on getting through the next 72 hours without any more deadlocks. Then, when I return, we can get closure on the cup."

"An intriguing strategy," Lyle said. "I hope it works."

"This is a tactical decision, not a strategic one," I corrected.

"Right," he agreed. "That's what I meant to say." Jarellen glanced at me and rolled her eyes.

"Remember," I said, "aim for the target. Build patience. Look for opportunities, not pitfalls."

I felt we had established a good framework for the next round. Jarellen accompanied me to the front door.

"I appreciate your work very much," she said as I stepped out onto the porch, "but I feel like there's a bigger problem here."

"Don't get discouraged," I said. "Think about Rule 46. Time is on your side."

"Maybe not," she said. "I think the real issue is that Lyle is an arrogant, self-centered creep. That's his personality, and it's non-negotiable. Do you have an answer for that?"

Everything suddenly went blank. The mental blackboard of my life experience was wiped clean. After a long and awkward pause I hesitantly said, "That's an interesting question." Then I walked back to the car and broke out in a cold sweat.

I feel better now. After careful analysis, I arrived at the realization that Jarellen is simply wrong. No other conclusion is possible. I mean, the idea of something that cannot be negotiated is simply inconsistent with the underlying procedural structure of my entire methodology. She'll be glad to know that, I'm sure.

Paperwork

Our company car stopped in front of a pile of wreckage that had once been a hardware store. I swallowed nervously.

"You didn't think the first day on the job would be easy, did you?" quipped Bob Bugelman, my training supervisor. He grabbed his clipboard and slid out from behind the steering wheel. The scene around us was like a surreal nightmare. A wide corridor of downtown Portland was pulverized.

Bob leaned back, took a deep breath, and smiled. "God help me, it's wonderful!" he beamed. "I love the smell of mass destruction in the morning!" Then he looked around sheepishly, realizing that some of the local citizens might be close by. "Sorry. Can't help it," he said, shaking his head but still grinning. "Godzilla is my weakness."

"What do we do first?" I asked. "Look for survivors?"

"They'll come to us," Bob said. "You'd think no one could live through such an ordeal, but they'll start emerging from under the rubble very soon."

He had barely finished the sentence before a man and woman climbed through the shattered front window of the hardware store. They looked around, hugged each other, and then started toward us.

"Let me do the talking," Bob said quietly. "I don't suppose you got much practice in field interview techniques back at the home office?"

I shook my head. "The company said it was more important to put all of our claims adjusters into the affected areas immediately," I answered. "They suspended the training classes and put my group on the next plane heading west. But I'm a fast learner."

"First thing you have to do is watch their lips," Bob said.

This seemed like an odd comment until the couple stopped beside us and began talking excitedly.

"Thank heaven help has arrived!" the man exclaimed. "We were so frightened! It was awful!"

"Godzilla was everywhere!" the woman added. "Smashing buildings! Crushing cars! Like toys!"

"Notice anything unusual?" Bob whispered as the man and woman continued their animated description of the rampage.

"They sound so guttural," I said. "And their lips keep moving even after they've finished a sentence."

"It's a phenomenon we call Far East Enunciation," Bob explained. "For some unknown reason, Americans who are terrorized by Godzilla and his rival monsters speak as if their voices have been dubbed into English from Japanese. It's totally amazing."

"He was huge!" the man continued. "Giant teeth! Angry eyes!"

"We were trapped!" said the woman. "Hiding like ants!"

"Well, you're safe now," I said, trying to be reassuring.

"According to the files," Bob said, "most people in this part of Portland were smart enough to buy monster damage insurance. So we need to find our policy holders and get the paperwork started."

For the next few hours we roamed through the demolished area, writing down names and addresses, and snapping photos of the incredible destruction. Bob kept up a steady, good-natured chatter with the citizens we encountered. He also enlivened the mood by whistling show tunes from *South Pacific*.

We finally took a break in front of a crushed Starbucks espresso outlet. There was a rich, smoky aroma from all the coffee beans scattered across the sidewalk. They made a distinctive crunching sound under our shoes.

"One thing I don't understand," I said, "is why Godzilla crossed the ocean and began attacking the coastal cities here?"

"Might be something to do with El Niño, that ocean current thing-a-ma-jig," Bob answered. "But who knows. Our job is to write the checks and get these folks back on their feet. Makes me darn proud to be representing the American insurance industry!"

"Help me! Please help! Come quick!"

We turned and saw a perspiring, corpulent man waving at us and panting with exhaustion. He was wearing greasy blue jeans and a t-shirt emblazoned with the slogan, 'I Brake for Ding Dongs.' He claimed that his carpet cleaning shop had been destroyed, and led us to the site a couple of blocks away.

A two-story building had been reduced to small pieces, but something wasn't right. "This is odd," Bob said. "We're outside the main path of destruction by several hundred feet. Godzilla doesn't usually make little side trips when he's on a rampage."

"Oh no!" said the man. "Not Godzilla! Mothra did this!"

"Mothra?!" Bob said, taken aback. "He was here, too?"

"Oh yes!" said the man. "Flapping his wings! The wind was like a tornado!"

Bob motioned for me to follow as we carefully picked our way through the twisted mess of wood, broken glass, and metal pipes.

"Looks pretty suspicious," he whispered. "Did you notice that his lips are in perfect sync with his voice?"

"Yes," I said quietly.

"You can't fake Far East Enunciation," Bob said. "It's a sure tipoff when someone is making a false monster claim."

"So how do we nail this guy?" I asked. Bob just winked.

"You know," he said loudly, turning back to the man, "Mothra usually smashes buildings flat into the ground, because the force from his giant wings comes straight down. But your place seems to have been blown apart, like an explosion."

Then I noticed a familiar, pungent odor. The timing couldn't have been better. "Hey!" I added. "I also smell ammonia. Do you think someone here was operating an illegal methamphetamine lab?" That was something we learned during the first week of training.

"No!" the man said, unconvincingly. "No meth lab! We were attacked by a huge creature! I am truthful!"

"Now that you mention it," Bob said, as if musing, "I heard that Megalon was also seen in this area last night."

"Megalon!" agreed the man, nodding. "Yes, that was it!"

"Did it look like a gigantic prehistoric turtle?" Bob asked.

"Of course! And so ugly!"

"Well, I hate to disappoint you," Bob said, "but the turtle monster is Ghidrah. Megalon is more like a giant cockroach, with cone-shaped razor devices for arms."

The man's face blanched, and he turned and began to run away from us with a clumsy, ox-like gait. Bob shook his head.

"I'll make sure the police hear about this," he said. "We always find a few creeps trying to cheat their way to a big payoff after a major disaster."

"That was great how you tricked him," I said. "Megalon! What a perfect set-up!"

"Hey, you were right on target with that meth lab angle," Bob replied. "I think we're gonna make a hell of a team! If you like this kind of work, I mean."

"I do enjoy the excitement," I said. "But it seems like it could get pretty depressing after awhile. I'm curious why you have positive feelings about Godzilla, anyway? He's such a frightening, destructive menace to civilization!"

"Oh, it's strictly personal," Bob said. "When he popped out of the surf in Lincoln City years ago and put Oregon on the map, the very first building he crushed was the beach house my ex-wife got in our divorce settlement. She and her boyfriend barely made it out of the hot tub in time. Since then, I've always felt really close to the big lizard. Kind of a male bonding thing, I guess."

"Gosh," I said, "aren't you setting yourself up for a terrible letdown when he's finally destroyed?"

"Destroyed by who?" Bob snorted. "Are you guys living in a plastic bubble at the home office? Godzilla's covered by the Endangered Species Act. The tree-huggers think he's helping restore the salmon runs up the Columbia River. And down in California the animal-rights crowd is so strong, they won't even let the Army shoot at him with rubber bullets!"

"I guess I should pay more attention to politics," I admitted. "Does this mean that we just have to follow him around while he smashes every town in his path, terrorizing innocent citizens?"

"You're going a little overboard," Bob chided. "That big green dipstick is just another force of nature, like a tornado. Folks in the midwest get ripped by twisters every year. Then they re-build and wait for the next one. Keeps the contractors busy."

"You make it sound like a normal routine," I said. "There has to be some way to break this cycle of monstrous violence. It's such a terrible waste of resources. Don't you ever lose any sleep worrying that one day these giant, hostile creatures may smash and destroy *your* home?"

"Ah, the idealism of youth," he mused. "Let me give you a couple of rules to ensure peace of mind. First, don't get married. And second, always be a renter. They can't take your house if you don't own one. I never get tangled up with real estate or women who want a commitment. And every night, I sleep like a baby!"

Give 'Em Hell

Not long ago James Nicotero, a Pittsburgh internist, got a call from his son Greg in California, who had a technical question: If a mobster were to crush the head of a stool pigeon in a vise clamp, would the eyes cave in or pop out?

Dr. Nicotero's opinion: Definitely cave in.

It wasn't a hypothetical question. Greg Nicotero is one of an elite fraternity engaged in the bloodiest rivalry in Hollywood: using advanced special-effects tricks to depict the most outrageous violence possible.

—*The Wall Street Journal*, March 27, 1996

"Joey," said Lou Bailey, my campaign manager, "we're in trouble. If the election were held right now, we wouldn't just lose. We'd get buried in a deep, dark hole. It's time to change strategy. We got six weeks left to make something happen."

"I'm willing to work harder," I said. "How about scheduling more neighborhood coffee talks? I think those have gone well."

"No, I'm thinking larger-scale than that," Lou said, and then he walked over to the door of the office, opened it, and leaned out into the hallway. "All right, we're ready," he said.

In response, two men burst through the doorway, shoving Lou aside and lunging at me. The first man was burly, with a fuzzy gray beard and tinted sunglasses, a green turtleneck sweater and a dark blue tweed jacket.

"Up against the wall!" he yelled, grabbing the front of my shirt and shoving me backward.

His friend was younger, with a wiry physique and a head of

thick black hair. Lou seemed amused as the two of them held my arms tightly and pinned me against the wall.

"Do you know what it feels like to stare at death?" said the burly man, holding a large hunting knife about two inches from my nose. I was too surprised to speak. "Your chances of winning are this close to being dead!" he snarled.

"Okay, fine," Lou said, calmly. The two men released my arms and stepped back. The burly man put the blade of the knife against his own stomach and shoved it in. I gasped.

"Hey, it's just a prop," he said, showing how the blade slipped back into the handle of the knife. "But we got your attention, didn't we? That's the whole point."

"Joey," Lou said, "this is Franz Benneker, the film director." The burly man pumped my hand vigorously. "And," Lou continued, "his special effects chief, Lazlo Toomey." The wiry guy nodded at me and gave a thumbs-up sign.

"You're probably familiar with their work," Lou said. "Their most recent feature, *Voodoo Nation,* won a blue ribbon at the European Fantasy Awards, and has just been picked up by HBO. They're now doing some political consulting on the side, and I definitely think they can help us turn this race around."

"Mr. Duncan," said Franz, "we've reviewed the latest poll results, and they're a catastrophe. Your opponent, Lester Hammond, is ahead by twenty points. Clearly, it's time for some dynamic action. You need to go on the attack.

"We have produced a sample TV commercial to spearhead your aggressive new approach. We believe Mr. Hammond is vulnerable in the area of children's issues. He has waffled on increased spending for education, and wants to reduce government aid to unwed mothers. So, how do we tell this to the voters?"

To answer his own question, Franz slipped a cassette into

the VCR we keep in the office. The screen on the video monitor flickered and then displayed the words, 'Joe Duncan/Hot Spot Productions/Children At Risk.'

"Is this—?" I began to ask, but Franz silenced me with a shake of his head and pointed toward the screen.

"DO YOU KNOW WHAT LESTER HAMMOND WILL DO TO OUR CHILDREN IF HE'S ELECTED TO CONGRESS?" a voice blared. The scene accompanying this ominous message showed the head of a young teenage boy clamped in a steel vise.

"Dear Lord!" I exclaimed, momentarily stunned.

"LESTER HAMMOND WANTS TO PUT THE SQUEEZE ON OUR KIDS," the voice continued, and the vise began to slowly clamp tighter on the kid's head. I put my hands over my face and peeked through the cracks between my fingers.

"LESTER HAMMOND WILL DESTROY SCHOOL FUNDING AND STOP ALL MEDICAL PROGRAMS FOR DISADVANTAGED BABIES. LESTER HAMMOND ISN'T JUST A BAD CANDIDATE. WHEN IT COMES TO OUR KIDS, HE'S A RUTHLESS, MURDEROUS CRIMINAL!!!"

I felt dizzy, and had to kneel down to regain my composure.

"Whatta you think, Joey?" Lou asked, businesslike.

"I, uh, I'm a little concerned," I said, taking a few deep breaths. I stood back up and looked directly at Franz and Lazlo.

"I'm not sure some of the stuff in that commercial is, well, factual. If you know what I mean."

"Ah, the eyes," Lazlo said, nodding. "It's true that in the real world they would cave in under the pressure of the vise. But we thought having them pop out of their sockets would be a more dramatic way to punctuate this particular message."

"No, I wasn't talking about the head crushing part. I mean,

that's also bothering me. But the stuff about Les Hammond being a murdering criminal—"

"Murder*ous* criminal," Franz corrected.

"Whatever. Uh, that isn't exactly a true statement," I pointed out.

"Joe, let's not get bogged down in semantics," Franz said briskly. "Think of the script as a marketing tool. You are targeting a specific audience. We want them to react to your opponent's name with negative feelings."

"Well," I said, "isn't there some other way to do that?"

"Oh, sure," Lazlo interjected. "Here's something faster-paced. We open with the teenager's head on the screen, and there's a shotgun barrel shoved into his mouth. And the voice-over says, 'IF LES HAMMOND IS ELECTED TO CONGRESS, OUR CHILDREN'S FUTURE WILL LOOK LIKE THIS!' And right then we pull the trigger."

"Mother of God!" I exclaimed. "Are you crazy?! We can't blow a kid's head off on television!"

"Oh, don't worry," Lazlo said. "It's not a *real* kid. See, we pack a mortar casing full of oatmeal, and mix in plenty of fake movie blood so the splatter effect— "

"Enough!!" I shouted. "I'm not ready for this!" I ran to a window, opened it, and stuck my head out. I felt flushed, and the fresh air brought some relief.

"Another option is to go with a simple decapitation," Lazlo offered. "That would definitely be the most cost-effective."

"Guys," Lou said, "could ya give us a minute here? Alone?"

After Franz and Lazlo had gone into an adjoining room, Lou spent a moment staring at the floor and clenching his fists.

"I know ya may not be too keen about this, Joey," he said, "but we don't have a lot of alternatives right now, and we sure as hell don't have much time. Hammond is getting too far ahead."

"Lou, aren't you worried?" I said. "About the fallout? I feel like we could get into a lot of trouble with this strategy."

"Ehhh," he shrugged it off. "It's a new era, Joey. Voters don't have the attention span anymore. Gotta shake 'em up any way you can. Hell, if we don't use Franz and Lazlo, I know three other candidates in this state who will snap them up tomorrow."

Just then I heard a commotion in the room next door. People were whistling and stomping their feet.

"What's going on in there?" I asked.

"Franz and Lazlo are showing the commercial to a focus group we recruited," Lou said. "I thought their reaction would help overcome any reservations you have about going on the attack."

The voices next door began chanting "Joe! Joe! Joe!"

"How do they know my name?" I wondered. "It was never even mentioned in the commercial."

"Oh yeah it was," Lou corrected me. "They inserted your picture and the words 'Joe Duncan' in about sixteen key frames during the spot. The images go by so fast, the human eye can't pick them up. The impact is totally subliminal."

Against my better judgment, I told Lou to go ahead and use the spot on the air. I also authorized him to produce the other version, showing the kid's head getting blasted by the shotgun. The next time I saw Franz and Lazlo was the day after the election. We met in the same office for a post-mortem. The mood was decidedly downbeat, because I had lost the election, by a mere two percentage points.

"Well, we almost pulled off a miracle," Lou said, trying to look on the bright side. "We just needed a little more time."

"Oh, save your bromides!" Franz sneered. "We would have

won going away if the TV stations hadn't strangled us with their damn restrictions. The spot only ran between midnight and 4 A.M.! How can they get away with that nonsense?"

"Ah, the station managers are always behind the curve on this stuff," Lou said. "They get jittery every time an irate mommy calls the switchboard with a complaint."

"But this is out-and-out censorship!" Lazlo said. "What happened to the Constitution? We had a message, and we were *not* allowed to present it to the full audience. So much for our precious freedom of speech. What a joke!"

"Ya live and learn," Lou said. "Next time we'll come out with our guns blazing right at the start." He winked at me.

"I suppose you're making a pun," I said. "Maybe next time the spot should have *two* kids getting their heads blown off."

"There isn't going to be a next time!" Franz interrupted. He stood up so quickly his chair fell over backward onto the floor. "I won't go through this humiliation again!" he continued, his hands shaking with anger.

"My friends told me this was a mistake, and they were right! I thought the election process had matured. I believed I could make a real contribution to the system. What a fool I've been!"

"Well, call us if you change your mind," said Lou.

"Not a chance," Franz replied, shaking his head. "Lazlo and I are flying home to Los Angeles this afternoon. It'll be nice to get back into a rational environment."

Lou wrote out their final paychecks. As the two of them were heading out the door, Franz turned back to us with a scowl. "I can usually remain emotionally detached from the projects I'm working on, but not this time," he said. "I never knew politics was so totally, thoroughly, unchangeably, *disgusting!*"

The door slammed behind him before I could agree.

Those Were the Days

The door to my office opened, and this woman blew into the room like a tropical storm. "I am Christine K. Hunsicker!" she announced. "And I am your worst-case scenario!" Then she leaned across the desk and briskly slapped my face.

"Ow!" I yelped. "What the devil is going on?"

"Are you Roland Cehalis, the building manager?" she demanded.

"I am him, yes. What's this about?"

"Are you responsible for the exhibit downstairs, the alleged representation of an American bachelor's apartment circa 1958?"

"Correct," I said. "You're referring to 'Joe's Pad.' It's my concept. It allows our visitors to experience a dynamic link with one of the most fascinating subcultures of the distant past."

"Liar!" she yelled. "Fraud!" She slapped me again, harder. "Christine K. Hunsicker says your exhibit is a complete disgrace," she continued. "Are you prepared to defend its integrity against my allegations?"

"There is nothing about 'Joe's Pad' that could be considered fraudulent," I said. "How dare you come in here and assault me!"

"I'm going easy so far," she said. "Things will get much more serious after we examine your little con-game up close."

She grabbed the lapels on my jacket and pulled me out of my chair and over the top of the desk. Her upper body strength was truly impressive.

"Don't try anything funny," she warned as we rode the

elevator down to the first floor. "I fully expect you to panic after I've presented my case."

"I can't imagine why," I said. When we reached the exhibit entrance, I gave a casual wave to Rhoda in the cashier's window and led my unwelcome guest through the door.

"Please keep your voice down," I cautioned, "so as not to disturb the staff or any visitors who come in."

"Forget that crap," she replied haughtily. "I assume the dipstick sitting on the couch is one of your employees?"

"That is Maynard Orndahl, who portrays Joe," I said, trying to maintain my calm, self-assured attitude. Maynard was leaning back with his feet propped on a small coffee table, reading a magazine. "How's it goin', boss?" he said cheerfully.

"Pretend we're not here," I said. "I'm just showing the exhibit to, um, a researcher."

"Yeah, you wish!" Christine snorted. She walked over to Maynard and grabbed the magazine out of his hands. "This seems highly unlikely," she continued. "A young, urban male in 1958 is sitting in his apartment reading *Boys' Life?* I don't think so!"

"Actual copies of publications from that period are extremely rare nowadays, and quite expensive," I pointed out. "I can't worry about specific titles on my budget. I think you're nitpicking on a very minor detail."

In response, her face turned crimson. She ripped the magazine in half, threw the pieces across the room, and slapped me again.

"Stop battering me!" I yelled. "It's inexcusable behavior!"

"Extremism in defense of historical accuracy is no vice!" she hollered back. "This whole display is bogus! Look at his clothes. A plaid flannel shirt, black denim pants, and leather hiking boots. He looks like he just came home from a lumber camp!

Couldn't you track down some corduroy slacks and a turtleneck sweater?"

"We can't have a discussion if you won't stop shouting," I whispered firmly. Then my worst fear was realized. A man and woman stepped through the entry door, along with three small boys. They looked like a family on vacation.

"Yo! Thanks for dropping in!" said Maynard. "I'm Joe, and this is my pad. It's a hip cat hangout."

"Did you hear that, kids?" the dad said, leaning close to his children. "They had funny talk in those days."

"What's going on right now?" the mommy asked.

"I'm just about to call my girlfriend on the telephone," Maynard said. "This is how young men and women spent much of their time developing personal relationships."

Maynard does a great job explaining the nuances of the exhibit to our visitors. He pretended to punch in a number on the keypad, and then spoke into the mouthpiece. "Hey, baby!" he crooned. "It's your main squeeze. Yeah, you're my hunka-hunka burnin' love. How 'bout we get together later and rock around the clock?"

"Golly," said one of the boys, "is he really talking to someone else?"

"No, dear," said the mommy. "He's just pretending. But in the old days, everyone had one of those little machines, and they were all connected by wires."

"Wouldn't so many wires everywhere be dangerous?" said the boy. "People would be tripping over them all the time."

"Oh yes," said the dad. "I bet people fell down quite a lot back in those days."

"Balderdash!" Christine interjected. "Save your worthless conjecture, sir!" The whole family was startled by her outburst. My stomach began to churn. "Also," Christine went on, "it's impossible for 'Joe' here to be using a push-button phone. In 1958 there was only rotary dialing. This is a bad joke!"

"Say, we paid for an authentic historical experience," the dad said with a worried tone. "I don't want to get cheated here."

"There is no need for concern!" I said firmly. "Thousands of patrons have found 'Joe's Pad' to be uniquely fascinating. And Joe is happy to explain his lifestyle, so don't be shy."

"What's going to happen next?" asked the wife expectantly.

"I'll probably listen to a few records on the hi-fi," Maynard said, "and then watch some TV. But each day is different. The life of a swinging American bachelor was never predictable."

"I can predict one thing," Christine said, examining the stack of albums beside the record player. "Good old Joe would *not* be listening to Herman's Hermits or the Dave Clark Five! The British rock craze didn't happen until the *Sixties*. This presentation is riddled with fallacious and misleading information!"

"Gosh, I'm really disappointed," said the dad. "Come on, kids, we're going to get a refund."

Heat was prickling up the back of my neck as the family silently turned and walked out of the exhibit.

"That's it!" I growled at the self-appointed critic. "Now you've gone too far! You're taking money out of my pocket, and you made those people feel bad! I'm running a feel-good exhibit here!"

"It's highway robbery!" she countered. "You're taking advantage of the rampant ignorance and apathy that permeates modern society, and just to line your own pockets! You don't care about what's true or false here. 'Joe's Pad' is a cash cow!"

"Hey, lighten up," Maynard said. "Nobody's perfect."

"Well, you're living proof of that adage," Christine replied. "Anyway, 'perfect' isn't the issue. This exhibit doesn't even qualify as 'barely adequate.' And where is the *bath*room?!"

"Beg pardon?" I said, taken completely aback.

"You left out one of the most vital elements of daily life in that period! Men spent excessive amounts of time in the bathroom preening themselves in front of big mirrors, shaving their faces and massaging various potions into their scalp. Where is it?!"

"All right, you got me on that one," I said. "But the expense of installing the pipes and tilework and such was horrendous. And besides, we genetically engineered body hair out of the human race a long time ago, because it was so inconvenient to maintain. I thought visitors would get squeamish seeing Joe shave. It would have required using simulated facial whiskers. For heaven's sake, this isn't a geek show!"

Then I heard a soft popping noise, and Christine flinched.

"Got her," said a voice. I looked toward the entrance and saw two men who had slipped into the room unnoticed. One of them was holding a plastic rifle, which was aimed in our direction.

"Don't be alarmed," the man said. "It's a tranquilizer dart." The pair ran over and caught Christine just as she began to sink toward the floor. She offered no resistance.

"Sorry to charge in like this," said the second man, holding up an impressive I.D. badge. "We're from the university. Christine left campus this morning without authorization."

"Did someone on my staff call you?" I asked.

"Oh no," said the first man. "All students now have locator chips implanted when they register. We keep track of everybody."

"Thank goodness you showed up," I said. "That girl has some very serious personality disorders. Is she ill?"

"No," said the second man, "but she's been victimized by an irresponsible professor. For some unknown reason, he attempted to raise the standards of performance this quarter. The kids were forced to read and discuss tremendous amounts of fact-based information about the past two centuries, and then suggest possible alternative outcomes based on hypothetical variations in cultural evolution. And he even took attendance before every lecture!"

"That sounds incredibly demanding," I said.

"Absolutely," said the first man. "Kids can't handle the stress of an educational environment that subordinates their feelings of self-worth in favor of higher test scores. America has become a gentler place since we dumped such rigorous academic methodology decades ago. You can see what it did to Christine. Her intellectual flexibility has given way to rigid, anti-social tendencies. Fortunately, she'll regain her normal personality once we get her on medication and counseling."

"And the professor?" I asked.

"He's been fired. And blacklisted," said the second man. "And we sincerely apologize for the disruption this has caused."

"Don't worry," I said. "One thing I've learned from studying the past is that there's no point arguing about something that's over and done with."

Seller Is Motivated

"I don't want to alarm you," I said to my associates as we stood on the front porch, "but this one could be a stinker."

I knocked on the door and waited. A light drizzle was falling. Leaves blanketed the front yard. The 'For Sale By Owner' sign in the lawn was leaning precariously.

But the dreary conditions had no visible effect on Milo and Helvetica Dunsmuir. They were smiling brightly, already looking for features of the house that could be incorporated into a snappy newspaper advertisement. Born realtors, both of them.

"How long has it been on the market?" Milo inquired.

"Eleven months," I answered, "and they haven't received a single offer. As usual, the owner thought he could sell it by himself and save on the commission. So I stopped by on an impulse last week, and he agreed to give us the listing. But I'm going to need help, and you folks always have good ideas." I knocked again, louder.

"Well, they should've called us right from the get-go!" Helvetica chirped. Her eyes sparkled with anticipation.

We heard the sound of a deadbolt lock turning, and the front door slowly swung open. A damp, musty odor filled the air.

"Thank God you've arrived," said the owner, Mr. Pearson, who appeared to be about fifty years old. He was extremely thin, almost brittle-looking, and was sweating profusely. "It hasn't been a good day," he added. "I sent everyone else over to my sister's place for a little while. This morning, when I woke up, my wife was being levitated. She was six inches off the bed."

"Oh dear," said Helvetica. "Is that something you can treat with medication?"

"We've tried everything!" Mr. Pearson replied, almost choking out the words. "Unholy evil is around us day and night! We just want to get away!"

"Do you mind if we take a look at the kitchen first?" I asked, whisking the Dunsmuirs past Mr. Pearson, who leaned against the door frame and began to weep softly.

"Listen," I whispered as we walked along the front hallway, "the Pearson family claims to have been terrorized by unseen forces for the entire six years they've lived here. It's an awkward situation for a home seller to be in, as you might imagine."

"Not to worry!" Milo said cheerily. "Adversity simply makes the final transaction more satisfying!"

I was encouraged by the clean, tidy appearance of the kitchen appliances. "It's nice and cozy in here," Helvetica said. She bent down and put her hand against the floor. "My, you could almost cook an egg on that linoleum! Is the furnace directly under this room?"

"We disconnected the furnace years ago!" said Mr. Pearson, who had quietly pulled himself together and rejoined us. "Sometimes it gets so hot we can't breathe! Like the fires of Hell!"

"I'm going to write down 'kitchen radiates special warmth' for the description in the multiple listing directory," Helvetica said, scribbling in her notebook. Milo, who likes the hands-on approach to home evaluations, walked over to the sink and turned on the cold water tap.

"Jiminy!" he exclaimed, jumping back as a red stream gushed out of the faucet. "Got a little rust problem in the pipes."

"That's not rust—it's *blood!*" Mr. Pearson said, clasping his hands together so tightly his knuckles turned white.

"Seems rather unlikely," I said, trying to sound conciliatory so as not to further agitate the poor man.

"Oh no," he insisted, "it's definitely blood. Human! We had it tested by a lab. They said it's Type O-Negative."

"Why, that's the universal donor!" Milo smiled. "You could probably sell it to a plasma center. We should at least mention 'potential income source' in the listing."

"I don't think there's enough to make it worth the trouble," Mr. Pearson said. "See? The water's running clear now."

"Let's take a look at the other rooms," I said quickly, turning off the tap. Just then a wisp of smoke curled out of the drain in the sink, and my nose detected the odor of burning flesh.

Luckily, plumbing problems in old houses no longer frighten me.

As we walked up the stairs to the second floor, a loud rapping sound erupted. It sounded like someone was pounding inside the walls with a large hammer.

"They're angry," Mr. Pearson said, looking at me fearfully. "They want you to get out of here!"

"The pipes at my house used to do that whenever I turned on the hot water," Milo said. "We'll have a plumber take a look."

The master bathroom was truly impressive. "This is wonderful," I said. "The shower looks brand new."

"We've changed the door seven times," Mr. Pearson said, "but the face just keeps coming back, over and over!"

"What exactly do you mean?" I asked.

"Look!" he said, terrified. "It's happening right now!"

As we watched, a strange misty outline appeared on the glass door of the shower stall.

"Bit of a condensation problem, I'd say," Milo offered. "Might need to put an exhaust fan in the ceiling."

"The image of Lucifer!" Mr. Pearson cried. "He's here!"

"Now hold on," said Helvetica, leaning close to the door. "I'd say it looks rather like a profile of Eleanor Roosevelt."

Mr. Pearson's face became even more terrified. "Same thing!" he cried, bolting out of the room.

"I told you this might be tricky," I said. "Just keep going without me. I'll try to help Mr. Pearson regain his composure."

I could hear the sound of frightened whimpering, which eventually led me to the closet of the master bedroom. Mr. Pearson was crouching down in a corner. "There is no escape," he said. "No place to hide. In this very spot, I was forced to have carnal relations with a female demonic entity. Not once, but on many occasions! Horrible green hair she had. Cracked, rotting skin. Foul breath. She delighted in my humiliation!"

"Mr. Pearson," I said, "I don't want to sound callous about your situation. But if you and your family were being tormented and degraded every day by hostile forces from the spirit world, why did you stay here so long?"

"El Pollo Picante," he said through clenched teeth.

"The Spicy Chicken?" I repeated. "Is that another one of the demonic spirits?"

"No," he said, raising himself back to a standing posture. "It's the Mexican rotisserie at the end of the next block. Their 'grande gordo' dinner combination special on Wednesday nights has saved the collective sanity of this family. I mean that literally. And it's right across the street from the Casablanca Theatre, which has a European film festival in the summertime. I've come to believe that Werner Herzog was a misunderstood genius of a movie director. Are you familiar with any of his work?"

"Not really," I lied. In my opinion, Herzog films are generally incoherent, and Klaus Kinski is a very disturbing actor. But I try to avoid discussing art or movies with clients.

"Hello!" Milo's voice called happily from somewhere downstairs. "We need to speak with the homeowner at once!" Mr. Pearson wiped his face with a handkerchief and we returned to the first floor, where Milo was brimming with positive energy.

"The wife and I have decided to buy this house!" he announced. "We intend to pay your full asking price. Problem solved!"

"Hail Mary, full of grace!" Mr. Pearson exclaimed, crossing himself as he bowed his head. Then he ran to the front door and flung it open. "It's not raining anymore!" he said, pointing toward the sky. "The veil of pain is lifting. I've got to tell my loving family the good news!"

As the sound of his footsteps echoed into the distance, I looked at Milo somewhat skeptically.

"Are you sure about this?" I asked. "I mean, it's not—"

"Tut tut!" he said, cutting me off. "No need for any reconsiderations. My spouse is in a state of total bliss. I've never seen her so overwhelmed by instant emotional attachment to a new home. Look, she's glowing with happiness!"

I turned and saw Helvetica approaching us from the far end of the hallway. Her eyes had become pulsating red orbs, and her lips were pulled back in a tight, feral-looking grin. Also, her feet were no longer touching the floor. It seemed like a good time for me to leave. I didn't want to say anything that might jeopardize the sale. Looking back, I caught a final glimpse of the pair, side by side and holding hands, as they slowly floated up the stairs.

Here's Looking At You

The little pharmacy was deserted when I put the sunglasses on. Casually, I glanced into the mirror mounted on the display rack.

"Hey, these aren't half bad," said a voice. Then I realized it was my own voice, except that I hadn't said anything. It was as if I heard myself thinking out loud.

I looked over at the old druggist standing behind the cash register. He was a short, wiry fellow with bushy white hair. His mouth didn't move, but his voice said, "Sonny boy, I wish you would buy something or take a hike, so I can close early."

"Well, if that's how you feel," I said, "maybe I'll take my business elsewhere." The old man looked startled, and then squinted at me.

"Oh, Je-*ho*-sephat!" he exclaimed, dashing out from behind the counter. In three strides he was beside me, peering closely at the sunglasses.

"Yep, those are the crazy lenses that let you hear what other people are thinking," he said. "Got a whole batch from my distributor in China about six months ago. Thought I had thrown all of 'em away by now, but I guess you got the last pair."

"Glasses that let you hear other people's thoughts?" I said. "And you just threw them all away?"

The druggist shrugged. "Nuthin' else I could do," he said. "They were a bust. Oh, I sold a few at the start, but people always returned 'em after a day or so. Go ahead and take that pair if you want. I won't charge you anything."

"Are you sure?" I asked. "I mean, the power to read minds

should be worth a fortune! Not to sound conceited, but I think I might be able to rule the world with these glasses."

"Great, I guess, if you like that kind of thing," the old man said. "I'm open from ten to six, Monday through Friday. You can bring 'em back anytime during those hours."

"Have you tried these?" I persisted. "I'd think they would be perfect for any businessman. You could read each customer's mind, find out what their favorite items are, and stock up on the stuff they like. What an advantage you'd have over all the other drugstores in town!"

"Yeah, it might seem that way. But people aren't thinkin' about the stuff you'd expect. Don't take my word for it, though. You just wear those for a few days. Then we'll talk."

As it turned out, I was back late the next afternoon. The druggist didn't seem surprised. He just held out his hand, and I gave him the glasses.

"Well, you were right," I said. "It was kind of a fiasco."

"I'm not going to gloat, but you can't say I didn't warn you," he said. "So tell me what happened. Who'd you look at first?"

"My mother," I answered. "She's always been very aloof toward me, but I never knew why, and I was afraid to ask. I wondered if there was a dark secret in the family history. Perhaps my conception was the result of some wild, irresponsible seduction, a one-night stand with a handsome but dishonorable sea captain. Things like that happen all the time on TV, you know."

The druggist nodded wisely. "Indeed they do," he agreed.

"So yesterday, when I got home, she was in the kitchen

cooking dinner. I set the table and did some other chores, and she was very quiet, as usual."

"And what was she really thinking?" the old man asked.

"In her mind, she kept repeating the same sentence over and over. And that sentence was, 'You can take Salem out of the country, BUT! You can't take the country out of Saaa—lem!' It was like a religious chant, or a mantra."

"I remember that slogan," the druggist said. "It's from the 60s, when cigarette advertising was still allowed on television."

"That's about when I was born," I said. "Turns out my mother quit smoking when she found out she was pregnant. And then I developed asthma, so that didn't help. And her unfulfilled craving for nicotine over the years caused her to withdraw into an emotional shell, buoyed only by the commercial jingle of the product she was unable to enjoy. I feel kind of guilty now."

"There's nothing you could have done," the druggist said. "Brand loyalty is so strong it can tear families apart. I've seen worse cases than yours. And what about your father?"

"He's always been cheerful, but lacking in concentration. He drifted from one job to another, and I thought it was because he was too smart for the kind of work he did. He claimed to have been a physics major at Columbia, but dropped out because he couldn't afford the tuition. It sounded to me like a great mind had been tragically stifled."

"And what profession did he pursue?" the druggist asked.

"He sold restaurant equipment," I said, "and he's also been a short-order cook. That's why I thought my mom might have fallen for a swashbuckling interloper, because Dad is so uninspiring."

"And when you looked into his mind, what did you discover?"

"He was humming a different jingle," I said. "It went like this: 'Two all-beef patties, special sauce, lettuce/cheese, pickles/onions, on a sesame seed bun!'"

"Ah, yes," the old man said, nodding. "I can't remember if that was for McDonald's or Burger King. Your father likes food, I take it?"

"Tremendously," I answered. "It's now obvious that's why he's never been able to get on track with a more lucrative career. He wasn't bored by his work. He loved it! It allowed him to visit restaurants all the time and sample their cuisine.

"Instead of thinking deep thoughts, he doesn't think about anything beyond his next meal. Most of his jobs these days are telemarketing gigs. He likes to nibble on snacks between calls."

The druggist clucked his tongue sympathetically. "You poor boy," he said. "If it's any consolation, I heard lots of similar stories back when these glasses first arrived. Everyone seems to have a cavalcade of unresolved issues involving their childhood, sibling rivalries, and embarrassing medical incidents. So tell me what happened next."

"I felt hurt and deceived," I said, "so I left the house and began walking the streets. I thought I might find some kind of higher truth by looking into the minds of complete strangers."

"I assume from the tone of your voice that it was not a successful quest."

"No, it wasn't," I admitted. "It seems that, at any given moment, most people are preoccupied with trivial and sometimes incomprehensible thoughts. It's hard to believe the world can function when everyone is so distracted."

"Do you remember anything specifically?" the druggist asked.

"Young women seem to dwell a great deal on new relationships," I said. "Many of them kept repeating, 'I wonder if he's really single?' or variations on that theme. Older women complained about physical discomfort. One phrase that came up several times was, 'I'll never go back to sticky paste or powders again!'"

"What about the men?"

"A whole lot of them are worried about the onset of gray hair and male-pattern baldness," I said. "Also, based on my survey, I estimate that at least fifty percent of men over the age of sixteen years old have fantasized about having a fling with Madonna."

"That sort of research is hard to generalize about," the druggist cautioned. "When I was reading people's thoughts, all the fellows were crazy about Sharon Stone. It was terribly unsettling, although I must say that I used to have similar thoughts about Sonja Henie. Is that when you decided to give up?"

"Actually," I said, "what happened was that I got so involved in listening to everyone else's mental blathering that I forgot to eat or drink anything, and I fainted after about seven hours. Someone called the paramedics, and I ended up in the emergency room at County General Hospital. And since I don't have health insurance, I'm stuck with a big medical bill. Stupid glasses!"

While I watched, the druggist broke the pair in half and tossed the pieces into a wastebasket.

"You won't tell anyone about this, will you?" I implored him.

"My lips are sealed," the old man assured me. Then he chuckled and shook his head.

"I suppose you're laughing at me now."

"No," he said, "I just remembered the old saying, 'A penny for your thoughts.' In most cases, that price is way too high."

Clean Up Your Act

"Look sharp!" I screamed as the men straggled in through the front entrance. "You are the biggest bunch of misfits ever to set foot in this establishment! Sergeant, line these men up!"

One of my assistants immediately stepped forward, and within moments the group was neatly arranged in a single row. Each man was wearing an orange jumpsuit with his name stenciled across the back in large block letters. And each one was carrying a large plastic basket filled with greasy, soiled garments.

"You're draggin' yer feet!" I bawled at them. "You're hangin' yer heads! And I will not have it! Do you hear me?!"

"Yes, sir!" they responded, more or less in unison.

"What did you say?" I replied, with an ominous tone.

"SIR, yes, SIR!" they yelled back.

"You're here for a damn good reason," I said. "Complaints have been filed against you. Citations have been written. In some cases you have been arrested and jailed. All because you cannot conduct yourselves properly in a public laundromat! You have exhibited behavior that our community will not tolerate. Thank God we have laws now that protect our citizens from your ridiculous and inexcusable behavior. I wrote those laws when I was on the city council. They were the first of their kind in this whole country! Because I know that getting your clothes clean is one of life's basic responsibilities. And if you can't get it done right, brother, you are gonna pull the rest of us down to your level. AND I WON'T ALLOW THAT IN MY TOWN!! Do I make myself clear?!"

"SIR, yes, SIR!" Some of them were already sweating.

"You all agreed to attend this boot camp as a way of avoiding court trials, which could have resulted in very severe sentences," I reminded them. "But, gentlemen," I went on, "you have never met anyone as severe as myself. Do as I say, and you'll be all right. If you screw up, I'll have your butt in the wringer faster than you can say Procter & Gamble. Are we all in agreement?!"

"SIR, yes, SIR!"

"Talk is cheap, gentlemen," I said. "Let's see who's ready to make some positive changes in their lives, starting right now!" The room suddenly turned into a beehive of activity as the men grabbed their baskets and began loading the machines. Some were tentative at first, but soon you could feel the collective momentum start to build. There's nothing more stimulating to the human spirit than the sound of quarters being shoved into coin slots, and the sudden gush of running water.

"Grakowski!" I yelled at a short, thick-necked taxi driver who was attempting to cram his entire wardrobe into a single top-loading washer. "What the hell is going on?"

"Just tryin' to get my stuff in the machine," he said with an innocent tone.

"Well, you're packin' it tighter'n a pickle jar!" I said. "You think the wash cycle is magic? You just close the lid and presto, no more dirt? Is that how it works?"

"I guess I never thought about it," he admitted, his bovine eyes staring lamely in my direction.

"Well it is isn't magic!" I shot back. "It's agitation! If you jam all those clothes in there, the blades can't possibly agitate the load properly. Your stuff might as well be sittin' in a hole in the ground! Didn't you read the material I handed out last night in the barracks?"

116

"Uh, I guess so."

"WHAT DID YOU SAY TO ME?!" I shouted in his face.

"Sir, I read the material, SIR!" he yelped, and he began frantically unpacking the overloaded machine.

"This is not a game, gentlemen," I said. "You have got to use at least a small part of the brain God gave you, and you have got to *think* about the *process* of getting the dirt out!"

I was getting warmed up nicely, and it gave me a heightened sense of awareness, like a sixth sense for trouble. I suddenly noticed a filmy white eruption bubbling out from one of the washers in a far corner of the room.

"Whose machine is this?!" I screamed, racing over to the washer just as more suds began billowing out from under the lid.

"Uh, mine, sir," said a stringy-haired punk named Wicks, a forklift operator at our local recycling plant.

"How much detergent did you put in there, Wicks?" I demanded. The suds had begun to ooze down the side of the machine.

"A cup, sir. That's what it said on the box."

"The *box* doesn't wash the damn clothes, Wicks! Don't ever do what they say on the damn *box*! They want you to use all the detergent in the world, so you'll run out faster and they can sell you *another* damn box! And this is what happens! Suds everywhere, the floor is a mess, someone's gonna fall and break their neck! And you standing there with your slack-jaw attitude. Half-a-cup, Wicks! That's all the soap you ever need to use! You didn't read the handout either, did you?! Go get a mop, and be glad I don't make you lick this up with your tongue!"

I had to pause for a moment right then and not lose emotional control. Oversudsing is a hot-button issue for me. I've suffered three separate hip injuries from slipping on soapy puddles at laundromats, and I have developed a zero-tolerance approach.

The stress can be especially hard on the older guys, so I wasn't surprised when a fifty-ish man wearing rimless glasses leaned over his machine and started sobbing. It was Hapgood Jensen, a local insurance salesman. I noticed that his clothes were still piled up in his basket.

"What is your problem, Jensen?" I inquired. "And don't tell me you can't figure out how the machine works."

In response, he held up a gray sweatshirt that was spotted with coffee, tomato sauce, and grape juice.

"Can I use bleach on this?" he sputtered. "Does it go with colors, or white stuff? I don't know these things! My wife always did the wash, and now she's left me for that gymnastics coach . . . " It was truly sad to see him dissolve into a baby-like state.

"You can cry me a river, Jensen, but you're gonna have to swim out of it eventually," I chided. "I'm sorry, gentlemen, but I've heard all the excuses! My wife left me! I'm on drugs! I have a learning disorder! It's all the same bad music! Gentlemen, let me repeat myself: clean clothes put us one giant step above the animal world! And if you can't, or won't, see your way clear to handle that responsibility, why then you might as well shuck your drawers right now and go live in a cave with Yogi and Boo Boo Bear! Because that's where you belong!"

"SIR, yes, SIR!" they responded, quite smartly. The atmosphere was reaching the perfect balance of simmering resentment toward me and silent remorse for the crimes that had brought them here. I knew we were making real progress when they started to interact in positive ways. Grakowski showed Jensen how to use a pre-wash stain remover on the sweatshirt. Then Jensen grabbed Wicks and stopped him from accidentally adding fabric softener to someone else's machine. They were looking out for each other.

And then came the reality check, like a slap in my face.

"Sir!" yelled one of my sergeants, waving at me from the entrance. He was holding on to a tall, wiry repeat offender named Waverly Buford, a guy who always gave his occupation as 'handyman.'

In my book, it was street slang for 'no-account deadbeat.'

"I caught this one on his way out the door, sir," the sergeant informed me. "He said you authorized it." I wasn't surprised. Buford looked at me with a sociopathic grin.

"Gentlemen, all of you, come over here!" I yelled to the group, and they gathered around us as Buford's eyes darted back and forth in their rodent-like sockets.

"It seems Mr. Buford here was going to leave us for awhile," I said. "He was just going to head out and leave his clothes sitting in the washer for God knows how long, while the rest of us sat here and cooled our heels." There was excited mumbling among the listeners, which is just what I wanted.

"Gosh, your majesty," I went on, "is that your standard procedure? I know the answer, Buford. You've got a reputation all over this county for leaving your clothes unattended. AND IT'S NOT GOING TO HAPPEN ON MY WATCH, YOU WORTHLESS BALL OF SLIME!" He jumped like I had poked him with an electric fork.

"You think you're so damn wonderful that you can go have a nice break during the hard part, is that it?! You don't care that someone else might need your machine when it's done washing?! Do you know how it feels to stand here and look at a machine full of wet clothes and wonder when the owner is coming back?!"

He gave me a little sneer, which is about what I expected.

"He thinks it's funny, gentlemen," I said. "He thinks his load of laundry is so far above the rest of you that we're basically ants under his royal feet. Well, Buford, the world doesn't work that way. We are doing our wash as a group, and we will stay here until hell freezes over if that's what it takes.

"Luckily for you, I can't think of a suitable punishment for your little antics." Now the mumbling turned angry, as the possibility loomed that Buford might be let off the hook. And that's when I sprang my trap.

"I can't think of any punishment," I said, "so me and my sergeants are going to go outside for a little while and let your peers decide what's right for you. Gentlemen, the slime ball is yours!"

I couldn't stop myself from grinning hugely as the door closed behind me and the men closed in around Buford. My wristwatch said it was almost noon. So much work still to be done. I was already looking forward to loading the dryers.

You Asked For It

It sounds ridiculous, but I can't remember much about the day television was destroyed. Everything happened fast. Recalling the details is difficult, and explaining them would be impossible.

There was no warning. I thought my cable system was simply experiencing technical difficulties. All the channels suddenly dissolved into a blizzard of electronic snow and white noise.

Later we learned that collective rage and frustration had erupted across the entire country in a wild orgy of destruction. Explosions lit up the sky as giant transmission towers were blown to bits. Sound stages in Hollywood were set on fire, along with the offices of every network affiliate in all fifty states. In the aftermath came suspicion, and then paranoia. It wasn't safe for anyone who liked television to question what was happening, let alone criticize the situation. We just went along.

When a mob of neighbors came to the front door, I handed over my set without protest, and smiled cheerfully as they tossed it into the back of a dump truck, which took it to a nearby landfill.

They didn't get everything, though. I hid some video cassettes under the floorboards, and I wasn't alone. Slowly, with great secrecy, small groups of us linked up. We met late at night, in unheated basements or cramped attics, to watch tapes of the old shows and remember better times.

The authorities got wind of it eventually. Somewhere along the way, they started calling us 'tubeheads.' The idea was to stigmatize our movement so that it would wither and die, but their smarmy tactic only made us more determined to resist.

We could not, however, overcome the overwhelming negative tide of public opinion. It was simply too easy to blame TV for glorifying violence, promoting sexual experimentation, and making teenagers think that Beverly Hills was a typical American suburb.

I was cleaning my VCR late one night when the phone rang.

"You've got to leave!" said a voice. "Someone informed on you! Don't take anything along. Just get going!"

"Go where?!" I asked, my heart pounding.

"Head for the railroad tracks, and follow them north. Don't stop until you come to the end of the line. Hurry!"

Moments after fleeing the house, I looked back and saw the flashing lights of police cars pulling into the driveway. Blind terror propelled me to the railroad yards, and by the next morning I was well past the city limits. Exhausted, I stopped to rest.

"You shouldn't be out in the open," said a voice.

"Who are you?" I asked, staring at the stranger beside me. He was athletic, tanned, and spoke with quiet self-confidence.

"I'm your traveling partner now," he said. "We're headed for the same destination. Let's get under cover, so they can't spot us from the air."

"Do you know where we're supposed to be going?" I asked.

"I've been told," said the stranger, "about a place where tubeheads live together in harmony. Our destiny is to preserve the heritage of television through this period of darkness and repression. When the American mind re-awakens, our knowledge will be the foundation for a new era.

"Until then, we must commit our favorite shows to memory. All videotape copies will be destroyed, so the government can't charge us with possession of illegal viewing material."

"What you're suggesting," I said, "sounds very similar to the plot of *Fahrenheit 451*. Did you ever see it?"

"Oh sure," he said. "Great film. Julie Christie was a fox. But the outcast people in that story had to memorize entire books. Our job will be much easier. Most people have already memorized lots of TV episodes without even trying.

"Of course, it also means that tubeheads will not have family names anymore. We'll simply have program titles. From now on, you can call me Wild Kingdom."

His knowledge of the outdoors served us well after the railroad tracks ended, and we embarked on a long trek through hilly terrain and thick forests. In the quiet wilderness, I had time to consider my own personal contribution to the new community.

After several days, we found a large clearing where dozens of people were camped in makeshift shelters of all types. A small man walked up to us and smiled pleasantly. He was wearing slacks and a casual sweater that buttoned down the front. "Welcome," he said.

"Hello," I replied. "I'm Mission: Impossible."

"Well, this is a beautiful day," he said, shaking hands. "I'm Mister Rogers' Neighborhood. And you know what? I like you just the way you are."

Shortly after my arrival, a meeting was held to choose a board of governors for the group. We knew that strong leadership tempered by wisdom and moral courage were essential to the survival of our movement. After much discussion, we elected Bonanza, The Waltons, and Victory at Sea. The vote was almost unanimous. The only sour note was a bit of grumbling from Happy Days and Charlie's Angels. They thought the board was

123

unrepresentative because we didn't elect any shows from the most recent decades.

Those first months, the atmosphere around the camp was energetic. Several sturdy dormitories were constructed under the supervision of This Old House. We enjoyed the comradeship of a frontier settlement. New arrivals were coming in daily, and it was believed that each of them would add something unique to the energy and diversity of the entire movement.

What I remember vividly is how much we learned about human nature as we shared our special talents in a spirit of trust and appreciation. "My husband wouldn't let me watch you," one woman confided to me. "He said Peter Graves was a lousy actor. What does a plumber know about acting? I finally divorced him."

I didn't think too much about my own personal future until one day when I was out collecting firewood with Highway To Heaven. We met another group that was gathering wild onions, and I caught the eye of a beautiful woman. Her thick black hair shimmered in the afternoon sun, and her auburn eyes sparkled at me.

"I don't think we've been introduced yet," I said.

"That's going to change right now," she said, giving me a provocative smile. "I'm The Twilight Zone."

We were inseparable after that moment, united by love and mutual admiration. Lying together in a grassy meadow, listening to the sound of birds chirping and the wind rustling in the trees, she would gaze up at the sky and say, "Tell me about the next mission."

It was our little game. "Good morning, Mr. Phelps," I would answer in an exaggerated baritone voice. "The man you're looking at is General Zek of the Karakian Army. Zek is so bitterly opposed to the peace treaty between the Kingdom of Karak and its neighbor, the Republic of Agir, that he has conspired with this man, Ismir Najiid, a munitions manufacturer, to provoke a war between the two countries instead of peace."

"Those made-up countries were always intriguing," she said. "Where could the Kingdom of Karak possibly have been located?"

"Somewhere between Turkey and Finland," I suggested. "Using your imagination was part of the fun. And I honestly believe that a short voiceover narration is the best way to grab an audience.

"Your program was brilliant in that regard. Tell me about the little guy with the thick glasses who loved to read."

"Witness Mr. Henry Bemis," she said with perfect Rod Serling inflection, "a charter member in the fraternity of dreamers. A bookish little man whose passion is the printed page but who is conspired against by a bank president and a wife and world full of tongue-cluckers and the unrelenting hands of a clock."

"The ending of that one always chills me," I said. "When the atomic bomb wipes out the city, and Burgess Meredith is finally alone with his books, ready to start reading, and he accidentally drops his glasses and they shatter."

My body shivered just thinking about it, and she wrapped her arms around me. I knew we were meant to be together.

Trouble was coming to paradise, however. Deer and other wildlife ravaged our garden plots one night. Gilligan's Island and I Dream of Jeannie were supposed to be on guard duty, but they had wandered off and gotten drunk on fermented huckleberry juice. When we found them sleeping in a wooded area, neither one seemed remorseful, or even embarrassed.

The fabric of any community will unravel if there are too many weak threads. We deluded ourselves into thinking that everyone shared the same intense commitment to the collective cause.

Other demoralizing incidents began to occur, mostly in the form of silly but destructive pranks. Pepper was sprinkled in barrels of drinking water. We never found that perpetrator. But I caught The Dukes of Hazzard and Married With Children as they were smearing pine tar on the toilet seats in the men's latrine.

Changes in leadership didn't help the situation. Victory at Sea and Bonanza had to resign from the board of governors due to illness, and they were replaced by Northern Exposure and Major Dad. It seemed to me that the overall mood of the camp was going slack.

One day a delegation showed up at the administration office, complaining that work details were too stressful. The Love Boat was the biggest malcontent, but he had lots of crybaby support from Family Affair and Petticoat Junction.

"You should take a cue from your own background," I said sternly to L-B. "Did Gopher ever walk up to the bridge and say, 'Merril, you're doing a lousy job running this ship?' No way."

L-B looked puzzled. "Who the hell is Merril?" he asked.

"Captain . . . Merril . . . *Stubing?*" I said deliberately. "Does that ring a bell? He's the main character on your show!"

"Oh yeah, him," he said. "Sure." I realized he didn't know the captain's first name. The next day, I began packing up.

"What's going on?" my beloved partner asked.

"It's over," I said. "All done. This whole concept is flawed. It isn't going to work after all."

We slipped away after dark, without telling anyone. The last sound we heard was a group of people singing around a campfire. It was a moment of painful insight, as the words from *Car 54, Where Are You?* echoed into the night: "There's a hold-up in the Bronx, Brooklyn's broken out in fights. There's a backup in Manhattan that goes clear to Jackson Heights."

"Did you hear that?" she whispered. "They have the lyrics all screwed up! It's supposed to say, 'There's a *traffic jam* in *Harlem* that's *backed up* to Jackson Heights.' How could this happen?"

"Our open-door policy was a big mistake," I answered. "It may sound callous, but some shows deserved to be canceled forever. Who needs The Love Boat, or McHale's Navy, or My Favorite Martian? Those shallow, lazy sitcoms dragged everybody else down to their level. I'm ashamed to be associated with them!"

Back in the big city, we rejoined mainstream society without causing any ripples of suspicion. My partner took the name Twyla. I couldn't make anything sensible out of *Mission: Impossible*, so I finally just called myself Slim. Work wasn't hard to find, and we settled into a lifestyle of drab conformity.

Our dreams and fears about the future all slammed together about two weeks ago. Twyla lost her grip on a soup tureen and it crashed to the floor. I rushed into the kitchen and found her sobbing in a corner.

"I can't hide it anymore," she blurted out. "I'm pregnant!"

"But darling, that's wonderful!" I said. "You shouldn't cry. This is what we've always wanted."

"There's something else, though," she said. "My intellectual grasp of the show is slipping. I seem to be forgetting key elements every day. I can't even recite the opening monologue for your favorite episode anymore. 'Witness Mr. Henry Bemis' is fine, but the rest is a blank! I'm frightened!"

"I understand," I said, holding her as she sobbed. "The same thing is happening to me. I've pretty well lost my entire first season. And I'm having trouble keeping track of all the co-stars in the right order chronologically. I think Lesley Warren was on the team before Lynda Day George, but I'm not sure! It's hard to retain so much information without any notes to study. And it'll probably get worse as the years go by."

"I thought we would have a special legacy to pass on to our children," she said. "Someday they'll ask us what television was all about. And if we explain that it was the greatest source of information and entertainment in human history, they'll wonder why it wasn't preserved, and protected. Then what will we tell them?"

"Only the truth," I said. "Some of us tried. We did the best we could, against overwhelming odds. And it just wasn't enough."

Flagrant Foul

The holding cell was enormous, and filled with a crowd of unlikely suspects. I was one of them, and I was petrified. How could this happen to a responsible, law-abiding citizen?

We had been playing a game of pickup basketball in the driveway, my son and some of his friends. And then, shockingly, I was on the ground being handcuffed. Stern police officers scowled at me in the paddy wagon. No one said a word until they shoved me into the crowded waiting area. "Sit down and be quiet," I was ordered. "Listen for your name. And don't make trouble."

It wasn't long until a voice said, "Eisenbarger, Richard N.!" I looked over and saw a guard motioning for me to come toward him. He was standing by the door of a small interrogation cell. Large glass windows allowed a clear view into the room. I could see a long metal table, several chairs, and an assortment of video cameras and TV monitors.

"Have a seat at the table," the guard said.

"Why have I been brought here?" I asked. "What did I do?"

"Yeah, yeah," he said, harshly. "Save it for the judge!"

The door closed, and for a moment it was blissfully quiet. I sat with my hands clasped together on the table, trying to keep them from trembling. Another door opened and two men entered. One of them was tall, broad-shouldered, wore three rings in each ear and a silver nose stud, and sported bushy blue hair.

"Wow!" I said. "You're Terrance 'Hot Toast' Talbert! The baddest man in the NBA!"

"True on all counts," said the other man, who was short and fat and wore an expensive three-piece suit. He was also holding my wallet and squinting at my driver's license.

"And you're Howard Kravitz," I said. "The sports agent. The one who got Hot Toast that big contract with our team."

"Uh-huh." He handed me the wallet. "Dickie," he said, "you're in some hot water right now. Look at this tape we secretly recorded while you were shooting baskets a little while ago."

He pushed a button, and the screen on one of the monitors brightened. I saw myself dribbling the ball with the kids. Then I jumped, turned completely around in mid-air so I was facing toward the hoop, and fell backward. Just before my feet touched the ground, I launched the ball. As it floated into the air, I sat down hard on the pavement, and executed a perfect backward somersault. I resumed a standing position just as the ball swished through the net.

"That," said Howard, "was an almost perfectly executed example of the Jelly Jump Rollover." It sounded like a compliment.

"That's *my* shot, man!" Hot Toast added.

"Yeah, well, I've been working on it," I said, trying not to seem like I was bragging. "Pretty good for a pickup game, huh?"

"Dickie," Howard said, "I'm afraid it wasn't good."

"It's *mine*," Hot Toast said. "I invented the damn shot!"

"And it's a patented move," Howard added. "Don't you read the papers? The Jelly Roll Jumpover is a crucial part of my client's creative expression. You cannot reproduce it without first obtaining proper licensing agreements."

"But I thought that law only applied to the other players in the NBA," I protested. "How can it affect what I do in the privacy of my own home?"

"Ah, but you were not *in* your home," Howard pointed out. "The pickup game was outdoors, in an area that is clearly visible to the public. The law is applicable under those conditions."

My heart was pounding. "Wait," I said. "Shouldn't I be allowed to have a lawyer in here with me?"

"Technically, yes," Howard said. "But I've already talked with the district attorney, and he would much prefer to settle this without a court proceeding. They're really jammed right now, so you won't make any friends by demanding a trial."

My face felt flushed with shame. "I am *not* a criminal!" I said, slamming my hand on the table. I stood up and walked to the big window. "This is crazy! My God, there's a troop of little Girl Scouts over in that far corner! What are *they* doing here?"

"Got nabbed at the campfire ring in Hideaway Park," Howard said. "Thought they could sing 'Puff the Magic Dragon' and 'This Land Is Your Land' without paying any royalties. Luckily, a representative from ASCAP was tipped off by an alert gardener."

"What's happening to our values in this country?!" I demanded. "We're treating decent citizens like common thieves!"

"If you're gonna launch into some 'victimless crime' tirade, save your breath," Howard said. "Look, Dickie, this is a *very* serious situation. In case you hadn't noticed, Uncle Sam doesn't manufacture things anymore. The steel industry is extinct. Cars, appliances, textiles, they're all going in the toilet.

"Our only real growth area is intellectual property, and we damn well better start protecting it! If we lack the backbone to enforce our trademark and copyright rules, well, we sure can't expect other countries to obey them."

It was all very upsetting, since I've never even had a parking ticket. Impulsively, I kneeled on the floor and began to recite, "Our Father, Who art in Heaven, hallowed be Thy name."

"Stop!" Howard shouted immediately. "You can't do that!"

"I'm not allowed to pray?" I asked.

"Not that one," Howard replied. "Paul McCartney owns it."

"No way! That's ridiculous!" I was feeling somewhat frantic, and totally helpless.

"I don't know all the details," Howard said. "It was a package deal, though. The Lord's Prayer, 23rd Psalm, a whole bunch of those really popular meditations were bundled together with all the major U.S. college fight songs. McCartney's a sharp cookie."

I bent forward and covered my face. "I don't want to cause any trouble," I said. "I just want to go home."

"You plead guilty to one count of misdemeanor trademark infringement, agree to some community service, and you'll be out of here this afternoon. Stay clean for a year, and it all comes off your record."

"What kind of community service?" I inquired.

"Personal appearances, mainly. At local elementary and middle schools. Students and staff need to know about the importance of observing these patent laws at all times. We want kids to grow up with respect for the legal system, right?"

"Gonna take us a while to get everybody in sync on this," Hot Toast said. "China laughs at our copyright laws. Must be twenty million guys doing the Jelly Roll Jumpover somewhere in Asia right now, and I'm not gettin' one red cent from any of 'em!"

"Here's something for you to wear at the schools," Howard

said. "It's got our campaign slogan." He handed me a t-shirt that was emblazoned with the words 'Don't Burn Hot Toast.'

"I'd just like to know one thing," I said. "How did you zero in on me for this infraction?"

"One of those boys in the driveway called the Hot Toast Hotline and gave us your name and address," Howard said. I must have looked surprised and hurt, because he quickly added, "It wasn't *your* kid, of course. God forbid that we, as a society, ever sink low enough that children are ratting on their own parents. The day that happens is the day I start thinking about a new line of work, and I mean that sincerely."

"I'm outta here," Hot Toast said. "Got to be at Gateway Mall in ten minutes for my book signing. Page me if there's a problem."

"There won't be any problem," I said.

After Hot Toast was gone, Howard looked at me and threw his hands up in the air with a grin. "Isn't he an amazing character? Very unique personality. And I'll tell you this: If America wants to stay Number One in the new world order, we'll need plenty more just like him!"

Be Our Guest

The lobby was empty. I rang the service bell next to the cash register. After waiting several moments, I rang the bell again, rather insistently.

A short, pudgy man wearing thick glasses stumbled into view from a doorway behind the counter. He was hitching up his pants, and his hair was askew.

"How in heaven's name did you get in here?!" he demanded, looking at me with a startled expression.

"I just walked in the door," I said.

"Just walked in?! From where?"

"A cab drove me from the airport," I said. "My flight was canceled, and the airline said they would pay for a motel room, so I told the driver to find me a safe place for a good price."

"Then you're in exactly the right spot!" said the man, suddenly receptive to my presence. "*Exactly* right! I'm the manager, and I was taking a power nap. However, before we begin the registration process, I have an urgent and disagreeable problem to resolve. Please remain standing right where you are, and don't move! — I repeat, DO NOT MOVE."

He hurried out of the lobby, vanished around a corner, and then reappeared less than a minute later. Panting from the effort, he resumed his position behind the desk.

"I just fired my chief of security!" he said. "Gave him his walking papers! Out! He has a wife and four children, and a dog that needs a kidney operation. But those facts are irrelevant.

"I simply cannot have people walking in here and surprising

me, the way you just did." He paused, and scowled with disgust. "The problem is," he continued, "all the really good security people have been swallowed up by the entertainment industry. Why should they dirty their shoes in my little business, doing honest work and protecting innocent travelers, when they can wear Armani suits and rub up against Madonna every day? I'm at a loss, truly. Now, how long will you be staying with us?"

"Just for tonight," I said. "One person, one room."

"Where's your luggage?"

"My suitcase was apparently loaded onto some other plane," I said. "The airline isn't sure where it went."

"Ah, the life of the modern traveler," the manager said. "I can assure you that *my* business is more committed to customer safety and satisfaction than any giant corporation. First, I need to see some identification. Then place both your hands flat on the counter. — Okay, now lift up your hands and step back from the desk."

It turned out that my palms had been resting on a thin sheet of clear plastic, which the man lifted off the counter and examined with a nod of satisfaction. "Very good," he said. "No smears."

"Did you just take my fingerprints?" I asked.

"Indeed I did," said the manager. "You see, I run the most secure lodging establishment in the entire tri-county region. There has never — I repeat, NEVER — been a death or serious injury in this motel. Although one guest did claim she was touched by an angel. I'm not sure how to classify that incident."

He slipped the plastic sheet into a machine that resembled a photocopier, closed the lid, and pushed a button. There was a humming sound, and then a long strip of paper began emerging from a slot in the side of the machine. The man tore off the paper and studied it with interest. "Excellent!" he said. "This confirms that you are not trying to register under an assumed name. And your record is spotless! We need more patrons of your caliber!"

"That's amazing," I said. "Do you check the criminal background of all your guests?"

"Absolutely," he said. "The machine can access fingerprint data bases for the entire western hemisphere. Helps me keep any wolves from slipping into the henhouse."

"I'm curious," I said. "Why does this registration form have a space for 'next of kin?' Sounds kind of ominous."

"There is always a remote chance that you may be victimized by some unusual phenomenon," he replied. "Falling objects from the sky. Spontaneous combustion. If the unthinkable *does* occur, I need to know who to contact, so that your funeral and legal affairs can be promptly and properly administered."

He opened another drawer, took out a key that was hooked onto a small brass disk, and placed it on the counter. The disk was inscribed with the equation '$2X + 2 = 66$.'

"To find your room number, solve for X," he said. "It shouldn't be too hard. You look like a high school graduate."

"I'm not good with calculations," I said. "Can't you just tell me the room number?"

"No," he said. "You'll feel better about yourself if we work this problem out together. First, subtract 2 from both sides of the equation. That means 2X equals 64. Divide both sides by two, so X equals 32, which is your room number."

"This is terribly complicated," I said.

"It's a precaution," he advised, "to keep your room from being ransacked if the key is lost or stolen. Mathematics is the first line of defense against criminal behavior!"

He bolted the lobby door and led me into the main corridor. "Do not leave the building without your key," he said. "All exits to outside areas will automatically lock behind you. You couldn't be in a safer place. Uh-oh, someone's gotten careless."

He pointed to room 25. The door was slightly ajar.

"Stand to the side," the manager commanded. Then he rapped on the door loudly. "Mr. Janowitcz! Are you in trouble? If I do not get a response in ten seconds, I will summon police officers!"

He looked at his wristwatch and began counting to himself. Then the door swung open, and a tall, bearded man stepped out from the threshold and gazed at us. He was garbed in an elegant purple satin robe and a large black turban. A glowing amber amulet dangled from a gold chain around his neck.

"I'm glad you're all right," the manager said. "Remember to keep all locking mechanisms securely fastened. The instructions are posted on your side of the door, right under the peephole."

The bearded man nodded, bowed gracefully, and disappeared back into his room without a sound.

"Is there some kind of convention in town?" I asked.

"You're referring to his clothing, I assume. My policy on all lifestyle issues is 'don't ask, don't tell.' We honor diversity here. Within the past year, this motel received top ratings from *Condé Nast Traveler* and *Rosicrucian Digest*."

Room 32 was clean and tidy. I took a shower and lay down on the bed. It wasn't very comfortable, so I called the front desk.

"I may need to change rooms," I said. "The mattress in here feels like a slab of concrete."

"That firmness gives your back crucial support," the manager answered. "Or you can use the futon that's rolled up in the closet. Place it in the far corner, behind the coffee table. That way, if a criminal somehow forces open the door and hoses down the bed with automatic weapons, you'll be outside the line of fire." When I shuffled into the lobby the next morning, two men wearing expensive blue suits were standing behind the counter.

"Checking out from room 32," I said, holding up the key.

"Just toss it in the wastebasket," said one of the men. "All the locks are being changed today. The motel is under new management as of this morning."

"Really?" I said. "That fellow with the glasses never—"

"Don't worry about him," the second man advised. "Like many people, he spent too much time worrying about trivial details, and never realized that your ultimate fate as an individual person is often decided by powerful forces beyond your control."

"That's kind of a scary idea," I mused.

"Perhaps. But it's the central theme of recorded history," the first man said. "By the way, the airline located your suitcase during the night. Here it is."

"Odd," I said, taking the bag. "I never told them where I was staying."

"We took care of that," the man said. "Our clients are very important to us. You have a nice flight home. If everything goes as planned, we'll be doing business with you again real soon."

"Okay," I said, nodding. "You're the boss."

He smiled. It was nice that we all understood one another.

Get With the Program

"I'm Sergeant Brickhouse," said the policeman when I opened the door. "Got a radio call on my lunch hour. Said you had some kinda problem here."

"Yes, there's been a break-in," I said. "I just discovered it this morning, so I'm not sure how much is missing."

"Well, let's have a look," the sergeant said.

"I think it happened last night, while I was visiting my girlfriend." We started walking down the hallway to my den.

"The snoopers like to poke around at night," he replied.

"Whoever did it came through one of the windows," I said.

"Yeah, windows is easy to break through." His grammar was disconcerting.

"Any idea what they got away with?"

"Some of my business and personal files are missing," I said. "That's all I've noticed so far."

We walked into the den, but before I could say anything else, the sergeant went over to my personal computer and sat down in front of the monitor.

"Shouldn't have turned this off," he said. "Sometimes we lose vital evidence just getting it booted up again."

"That's where they got through," I said, pointing toward the cracked pane of glass a few feet away. But the sergeant wasn't paying any attention to me. He was fumbling around with some of the electrical cords on the computer.

"How did you have your files stored?" he asked.

"In boxes," I said. "Not very sophisticated, I admit."

"Never heard of boxes," he answered. "Is that something Microsoft puts out?"

"What are you talking about?" I said.

"Where the hell is your modem?" he said, sounding irritated. "Did they steal that, too?"

"I've never had a modem," I said. "Why is that important, anyway? Look, don't you want to see where they broke in?"

"How could they break in when you don't have a modem?"

"They forced open a window! Right there!" I walked over and pointed to the glass.

"You mean someone physically came into this house?" the sergeant said, taken aback. "That's really disturbing."

"And I kept all my important files in cardboard boxes along that wall," I added. "Some of them are missing."

"You had paper containers just sitting on the floor in here? Man alive, I've heard about people like you." He shook his head. "Are there oily rags piled up in a corner, too?" He looked around the room, genuinely concerned.

"Sergeant," I said, "my home environment has been violated. Aren't you going to dust for fingerprints or something?"

"Look, there's been a mixup here," he said. "I'm with the 'tech-crimes' division. You need to talk with the officer who handles 'material theft/offline.' He's out sick today. Frankly, we don't get many calls like yours anymore. Thank God."

"Hold on here," I protested. "I pay taxes, too, you know."

"Wow, look at this!" he exclaimed, holding up one of my floppy disks.

"MS-DOS Version 2.11. You know how much you could get for this at a collectors show?"

"I can't sell that," I said. "I use it almost every day."

"I gotta hit the can," he said, changing the subject. "This place have indoor plumbing?" I detected a hint of sarcasm.

"Of course it does!" I was getting pretty irate. "Go back up the hall, first door on the left."

A few minutes later he came out of the bathroom and started for the front door.

"Is that it?" I said. "You're not even taking a report?"

"Look, pal," he said, softening a bit, "you have to understand. I got out of the legwork business years ago. People who need help usually just e-mail their crime reports right into the precinct database. I don't know where you've been for the past decade, but here's my advice: Take a few extra bucks and upgrade your system. Find yourself a nice second-hand modem. Go online. In other words, pal, GET A LIFE."

Payback Time

Nothing feels better than laughing with pure joy, especially when the joy comes from seeing fundamental beliefs vindicated. My favorite laughing spot these days is a fence post alongside the entrance gate at River Glen Farm. I go out there every Saturday to buy fresh produce. Boone, the owner, has a great pricing system. Right now I can get a sixty-pound sack of his best Idaho russets for two uncirculated 1964 Kennedy half-dollars.

"I'm startin' to wonder how many of those Kennedys you got, anyway?" he joked on my last visit.

"Just keep the spuds coming," I replied, grinning.

A green Volvo station wagon appeared over a nearby hill and slowly approached us, bouncing along the rutted dirt road.

"Looks like a family," I said. "Man and woman in front. Two kids in back. Should be fun."

"The Volvo crowd is always a kick in the pants," Boone added.

The car pulled to a stop near the gate. The driver looked like a successful banking executive, with his blow-dried hair and wire-frame glasses. All four occupants seemed extremely nervous.

"Might you have any supplies for sale?" the man inquired. "We were told that farmers sell direct to the public out this way."

"Depends on what you plan to pay me with," Boone said, picking up a piece of straw and chewing on it with studied indifference.

The man slid out from the driver's seat, walked to the back of the station wagon, and opened the rear door. I noticed that the storage area was covered with a blanket. He lifted the blanket, pulled out a small wooden box, and came toward us.

"Perhaps this will interest you," he said, opening the box. It was a display case filled with small, shiny disks. Boone and I took one glance and doubled over, our lungs heaving.

"What is so funny?!" the man said indignantly.

"Commemorative space medallions from the Franklin Mint—!" I gasped. "Such a deal!" Our jovial howling was most impolite.

"These medals are real sterling silver!" the man said. "That's what you people want, isn't it?"

"Look, mister," Boone said, catching his breath and wiping tears from his eyes, "I can tell you're new at this, so let me explain a few things, okay? Farmers may live close to the land, but we aren't complete rubes. The underground economy has a few simple guidelines. Me, I only take legal tender U.S. coins, gold or silver, uncirculated or proof quality. What you got there in that fancy display case is a big joke, which explains why we're laughing so hard."

"But it's precious metal!" the man insisted. "And a limited edition. Only twenty-thousand sets were authorized. The brochure said it was going to be highly sought after by collectors!"

"By God, that musta been some brochure," Boone quipped.

I turned away and held my sides. The sound of our mutual cackling rippled out across the valley.

"Can we see what else ya got in the car there?" Boone asked, moving toward the rear door. "Just so as to save some time?"

Without waiting for an answer, he threw aside the blanket to reveal an odd assortment of potential barter items. I could see a few boxes of glassware, stacks of old LP record albums, and some framed oil paintings. Boone reached into one of the boxes and let out a derisive whistle.

"Can you beat this?" he said, handing me a small, flat object.

"Hey, we're in clover!" I snickered. "Collector plates from the Bradford Exchange! I always wondered who bought these things."

"They actually belong to my sister," said the man. "Are you interested? The one you're holding is the Wizard of Oz 50th Anniversary issue. It comes with a certificate of authenticity."

"She might as well use it for a dog dish," Boone said. Then he began rummaging in a canvas bag, and discovered that it was stuffed with neatly wrapped bundles of crisp new $20 bills.

"Is this your weekly salary?" Boone asked, flipping through one of the bundles like the pages of a dime novel.

"Less than half a week, actually," the man said. "We get paid every other day. I don't suppose you'll accept cash for your goods."

"Nah," Boone said emphatically. "Only thing you can do with paper money out here is grind it up for cattle feed."

"I have a lot of savings bonds, and treasury notes," the man said, holding up two thick manila envelopes. "All backed by the full faith and credit of the U.S. government."

"Uh-oh," I chortled. "Is that a promise or a threat?"

"I resent your demeaning attitude!" the man snapped. "I'm just trying to do right by my family! Our money is virtually worthless, and the supermarkets are low on everything. I've worked hard and made responsible investments during my adult life, and now it's come crashing down. But instead of helping your fellow citizens in this crisis, you mock us!"

"Bottom rail on top now," Boone said, unmoved by the outburst.

"What the hell is *that* supposed to mean?"

"It means," I said, still smiling, "that some folks, such as myself in particular, could not be happier about the situation.

"All you bull market joyriders had lots of fun while the Dow Jones average ran wild. Seemed like the good times would last forever. But some of us stuck with old-fashioned hard money. We were poking around flea markets and estate sales, filling up shoe boxes with silver dollars and small change while you bigwigs stuffed your portfolios with shares of IBM and Microsoft.

"You called us 'gold bugs,' 'doom-and-gloomers,' and every other name in the book. We warned you, though. We said the whole Wall Street game was a house of cards. And you weren't listening."

"That's not true!" the man interrupted. "We listened. But we never thought it could really happen! It's just not logical for the agrarian sector to have so much power over the lives of affluent, well-educated Americans!"

"Jeffersonian populism *does* have painful side-effects," I sneered. "I wish I could've seen your face when the religious fanatics in the Middle East shut off the oil. And I bet you were sweating buckets when those giant solar flares blew out your whole global network of communication satellites."

"It could have turned out all right!" the man argued. "But people with backward ideas like you caused everyone else to panic!"

"Oh yeah, blame the victim," I retorted. "Look, pal, when the currency collapses and hyper-inflation sets in, societies throughout history have fallen back on gold and silver coins as the most reliable standard of exchange. Real wealth comes from the ground. You can't create it by turning on the printing presses.

"Now you and your Freemason/Big Business/World Government cohorts are in deep yogurt without a paddle. So take that and stick it in your ditty bag!"

"Poppa," said one of the little boys in the back seat, "what's a ditty bag?" The man just stared blankly toward the horizon.

"It's a nautical term, son," I said to the boy. "Sailors were issued cloth sacks for storing personal gear. The lore of the sea is quite fascinating."

"Please don't lecture my children," the man said, regaining his voice. "They're not going to have maritime careers."

"Don't be too sure about that," I replied. "Economic hardship has always been the navy's best recruiting tool."

"Excuse me, sir," said the boy, hesitantly. "Do you want to look at my old dimes? They might be worth something."

"Joey, what're you talking about?" the man said, surprised.

The boy reached under his seat and then handed Boone a small, blue cardboard coin album entitled 'U.S. Dimes 1946-1964.'

"I didn't know you had a hobby," the man said. "Where did you get those, anyway?"

"They were in grandfather's house," Joey said. "He had a secret compartment in that big wooden desk. He said I could have his whole collection someday. But then you sold all the furniture in the house right after he died."

"Well, thank goodness for children and old folks," Boone said. "Now we can do some business. Although I do wish these weren't Roosevelt dimes. He outlawed private ownership of gold, you know. Tried to pack the Supreme Court, too. A power-crazed egomaniac!"

"I really don't know anything about that era," the man

said. "I just want to get some fresh fiber into our diet. We've been eating Crisco sandwiches for the past four days."

"We'll get you fixed up," Boone said. "Also, I'm takin' volunteers right now for help with the summer crops. You'll get a daily wage, plus discounts at the farm store. Just gimme your name and phone number." He held out a pen and a tablet of lined paper. The man flipped through several pages that were already filled.

"Cripes!" he said. "My boss and three neighbors are already on this list!"

"You city folks don't seem to communicate with each other very well," Boone said. "Workin' in the open air is a good way to change that. And you'll be drinking only pure, fresh, un-fluoridated spring water."

The man took the pen from Boone and signed the list. I struck a match on my shoe and lit up a Chesterfield. The man gazed at me with a flat, hollow-eyed stare. I took one drag, stepped toward him, and handed over the cigarette.

"Thanks," he said, placing it between his lips.

"Mommy," Joey whispered, "I didn't know Daddy smoked."

"Don't worry, son," I said. "Your dad is trying to do the right thing. Someday you'll understand."

Don't Touch That Dial

"I honestly believe," said the producer, "that the changes we're making will have a positive effect in the long run."

My girlfriend, Beryl, stared at him in disbelief. "This is totally ridiculous," she said. Then, turning to me, she added, "Darius, are you just going to sit there and do nothing?"

The only response I could think of was 'yes,' but fortunately I didn't have time to verbalize it.

"It's not up to him," said the producer, sipping from a bottle of kiwi-flavored mineral water.

"He's my significant other," Beryl said angrily. "That makes him a rather important element of the discussion, right?"

"When we go back on the air, he'll be your 'insignificant' other," said the producer. "Now listen to me, both of you. We all knew, right from the start, that 'Totally Real Life' would not be an easy project. A typical urban couple, selected at random, no prior TV experience, with cameras following them everywhere. However, remember this key fact: You agreed to co-operate with all aspects of production, including possible changes in plot structure and/or character development. It's in the contract."

"But you're kicking me off the show!" Beryl protested.

"Not true," said the producer. "We're getting you into your own apartment, across town, and we'll try to work out a sched-ule of semi-regular appearances. Everything's cool. Trust me."

"The movers are here!" We turned and saw the associate producer standing in the doorway. She was a blonde, brittle, cheerless woman who always carried a thick writing tablet and scribbled copious notes during every conversation. "Come this way," she said, and two men in blue coveralls appeared behind her.

"Great," said Beryl, curtly. "I've heard 'trust me' before. It's TV talk for 'drop dead.' Excuse me while I pack my things!" She walked into our bedroom, and in a moment we heard the sound of a cello screeching out a halting rendition of "Yesterday." The producer walked over and closed the bedroom door when the movers began carrying out furniture tagged with Beryl's name.

"That is our whole problem in a nutshell," the producer said to me, frowning. "She's become reclusive, which makes your relationship boring. And this sudden fascination with musical instruments is preposterous. The ratings went in the tank the day she came home with that damn cello."

"She's always been very intense," I said. "It might have been less awkward if you had given us some warning about this decision."

"You want to know what awkward feels like?" he said, almost sneering. "Awkward is getting pounded by re-runs of 'Alf'! That's what happened to this show last season. The only audience segment that held steady was teenagers who never finished high school."

"I wondered about spending more time with my shirt off," I suggested. "I've ordered one of those exercise devices — I think it's called the 'Ab Cruncher.' How about a workout segment?"

"Not likely," the producer said. "If you have any more suggestions, just put them in writing and I'll read them later. Now I'm going to run through these other revisions fairly quickly, so just listen. I want to be sure you're clear on each one."

"Comin' through!" shouted one of the movers, pushing a hand truck toward the bedroom. The odor of manual labor was becoming powerfully evident, which only added to my feeling of ennui.

Then, for the first time in my life, I thought I was experiencing a hallucination. My stepmother, who spends most of her time lying in the sun and slamming downing highballs at her Palm Springs condominium, walked into the room unannounced. She was wearing a faded Los Angeles Dodgers warmup jacket, and leading a small, rodent-like dog on a braided leather leash.

"No blare of trumpets for me?" she sniffed. "Typical."

"What in heaven's name is *she* doing here?" I demanded, backing away and then crouching behind one of the chairs.

"Delna is going to be living in the apartment next door for awhile," the producer informed me.

"No," I answered, shaking my head. "That won't work."

"Just like your father," she said breezily. "The men in this family always try to hide when they don't get their way."

"You gave him a fatal heart attack because you're such a pushy, self-absorbed cow!" I yelled, still hunkered down so she couldn't see me. "The Holstein from hell!"

"Don't go over the top just yet," the producer admonished me. "Save your energy for the show. This is exactly the kind of dynamic tension we need to bring the viewers back."

"I'm taking Hamlet for a walk," the she-devil said, snapping the leash and prancing out the door. I raced into the bathroom and began splashing cold water on my face.

"You can't do this," I said to the producer. "Can't! Do this!" The hostility I experience in the presence of my stepmother often triggers episodes of obsessive-compulsive behavior,

152

and the first indication of trouble is when I start repeating the last few words of every sentence.

"Rest assured, nothing is set in stone," the producer replied. "But we think this is a good opportunity for exploring the nuances of inter-generational relationships in a family context. The idea sparked a lot of excitement at the production meetings."

"It sounds to me like you're just exploiting an unpleasant situation," I said. "Unpleasant! Situation!"

Grabbing a towel to mop my still-wet face, I hurried back into the living room and began hopping in a circle on one foot while yelling, "Ow! Ow! Ow! Ow! Ow! Ow! Ow!" For some reason, seven quick barks will usually break the obsessive speech pattern.

Dizzy, I stretched out flat on the floor. "Sorry," I said. "This is all very disorienting. I'm not sure where the TV show ends and my own private life begins anymore."

"You'll drive yourself crazy if you start engaging in that sort of philosophical hair-splitting," the producer said. "Just let your actions flow naturally, depending on the circumstances that may arise in each particular scene. I'm feeling very confident, based on what I've observed so far."

"Hey. I don't hear anything," I said. The place was suddenly quiet. I got up and walked into the bedroom. "Beryl's gone!" I exclaimed. "How could she leave without talking to me?"

"You were in the lavatory," said the associate producer, scurrying past me to grab a small cardboard box the movers had overlooked. "I asked her if she wanted to say goodbye, but she just put the cello under her arm and went out to the truck. I'll be back after we unload this stuff at her new place." She hurried out of the apartment and slammed the door behind her.

"Three years together," I mumbled. "Where does the time go?"

"You're ready for a change, Beryl's ready for it, and we're all gonna be better for it," said the producer.

There was a loud knock on the door. "*Now* what did she forget?" I said, expecting to see the associate producer. But when I opened the door, a beautiful model wearing a skimpy two-piece bathing suit was standing in the hall holding a large, flat box.

"It's the Bikini Pizza girl!" I said. The woman handed me the box, pinched my ear playfully, and sauntered brazenly into the living room. I was transfixed.

"I thought we could use some lunch," the producer said. "And you're going to be ordering a lot of these pies. When we showed clips from last season to our focus groups, everyone commented favorably on the visit from the Bikini Pizza delivery girl. So we want her stopping by as often as possible."

It sounded promising. But so far we haven't developed much personal chemistry. Every time the Bikini Pizza girl shows up, my stepmother seems to appear out of nowhere and chases her out of the apartment. Then I lose my temper, and the whole scene dissolves into a shouting match. Which, of course, she thrives on.

The killer headaches started about a month into the new season, and nobody can figure out what my problem is. X-rays and the CT scan were all negative. But the ratings took a huge jump, and the producer told me that a medical mystery is the best possible way to establish viewer loyalty.

He did agree to let me check into a private clinic for some sophisticated neurological testing, and said I could have a break from the cameras for a few days. I was concerned that we might lose momentum. Our fan mail is coming in by the truckload.

"Don't worry," the producer said. "Delna can carry the load by herself for awhile. Call me when your tests are finished."

I've been watching her antics every day on the TV in my private room, and the relentless outpouring of sarcasm and verbal venom from her tobacco-scarred larynx is truly riveting. She's been out shopping around for a Harley-Davidson, which has caused considerable anguish for the local motorcycle dealers.

The doctors here don't think my problem is serious. They suspect a pinched nerve in my neck. Everyone on the staff has been wonderful. I thought it would be nice to have the cameras rolling when I'm discharged in a few days.

The associate producer didn't jump at the idea, however. "We're taking the show on the road for awhile," she said over the phone. "Delna just bought a great touring bike, a new BMW-K75. She'll be heading into the wild blue yonder tomorrow."

"For how long?" I wondered.

"We're going to play it by ear," the associate producer said. "If the ratings keep going up, we'll just burn rubber every day."

"What am I supposed to do while The Mad Cow Traveling Circus is on tour?" I asked snidely. "I thought this was *my* show."

"The producer wants you to sit tight until we get back."

"I want to talk with him," I said. "Talk! To him!"

"He's scouting locations," the associate producer replied. "Look, just relax. The checks will keep coming every week. And you can finally have some quality time with the Bikini Pizza Girl."

"Okay," I said cautiously. "But I won't wait forever."

"Everything's fine," she said. "I'll call you. Trust me."

The Creamy Smooth Rescue

"Hang on, Skeeter!" Poppy yelled, gripping the steering wheel so hard his knuckles turned white. "We're almost at the target. You and your sister will be re-united at last!"

The long search was over. Our customized Subaru four-wheel-drive sport sedan was speeding uphill on a narrow, un-marked blacktop road in rural New England.

I looked into the back seat. Konrad, the journalist from Argentina who was riding with us, looked carsick.

"We are soon to stop driving?" he asked hopefully.

"Yes, very soon," I said.

"Telling to me again, some details," Konrad said, holding his tape recorder up to my face. "Bad man is holding your sister?"

"Right," I said. "Very bad man. She is taken years ago." I was lapsing into the crude English that Konrad favored. "Now, Grandpapa and I make justice! Tina libertad!"

"There it is!" Poppy exclaimed as we reached the crest of the hill. The road led down into a narrow valley, straight toward a low rectangular building surrounded by a chain link fence. A single guard was visible in a small booth at the front gate.

"This man," Konrad said, haltingly, "is — how you describe?"

"An evil cosmetics executive," I said. "Look, do you want me to go through the whole story again?" He nodded emphatically, so I quickly summarized our strange family saga. Central to the story is my father, a daring aviator, who perished when his stunt plane malfunctioned at an airshow on the very day his wife discovered she was carrying twins.

In poor health, she struggled to raise Tina and me with help from her own father, Poppy. Then, when we were barely five years old, she met The Swine.

His polite and gracious courtship was all a scheme. When Mom passed away, Poppy tried to get custody of us. The Swine cut me loose as a compromise. He only wanted Tina, and when the ink was dry on the final settlement, they disappeared.

"So, these many years you are searching," Konrad said, and I nodded.

"Also," he continued, "you have the psychotic links?"

"*Psychic* links, yes!" I shouted over the roaring car engine. "My sister and I are twins! We feel the same things!"

The paranormal bond was both fascinating and frightening. Sometimes, without warning, I experienced strange sensations on my skin. It might be a cool tingling across the shoulders, or wet stickiness on my face and neck. What, I wondered, was The Swine doing to Tina to cause these peculiar epidermal incidents?

"Ach!" Konrad exclaimed, shaking the tape recorder. "The machine iss malfunctionary! I take notes instead!" He tossed the recorder aside and reached into his briefcase for a writing tablet.

I leaned toward Poppy and cupped my hand over his ear. "Why couldn't we get an American reporter to come with us?" I asked.

"Nobody here would give us any money up front!" Poppy answered. "I haven't told you how much this escapade is costing. Luckily, the South Americans love this kinda story. Missing child, sinister capitalist stepfather, supernatural bonding. His magazine bought first serial rights for the whole western hemisphere."

Just then, I saw a small metal sign posted beside the road. As our van flashed by the sign, my eyes read the words clearly:

WELCOME TO THE POND'S INSTITUTE

Poppy didn't slow down as we crashed through the wooden gate at the entrance booth. The guard seemed paralyzed with astonishment. The road led us through a spacious parking lot, and then to a circular turnaround area in front of the main building. Poppy screeched to a halt at the curb. "Gott in himmel!" Konrad gasped. "My stomach is feeling to upchuck!"

He began retching violently as Poppy and I jumped out and ran toward the heavy glass doors. Each of us carried a nylon tote bag filled with smoke bombs and concussion grenades.

"I asked him this morning if he wanted some dramamine," Poppy snorted. "These modern reporters are nancy boys. Ed Murrow never tossed his cookies on a big story!"

The front doors swung open easily, and we were immediately spotted by a male receptionist who was sitting at a large desk.

"Excuse me! One moment!" he shrieked. "We don't allow anyone in here without an appointment! Not even Joan Collins!"

In response, I grabbed an aluminum baseball bat from my tote bag, ran to his phone console, and smashed it into small pieces.

"Coffee break time!" I yelled, yanking him out of the chair. It didn't take more than a second for his furiously pumping legs to carry him away from the scene.

The reception desk was positioned directly in front of two wide corridors. Poppy headed toward the one on the right, and I went left. We had secretly obtained blueprints of the floor plan, and we knew that each corridor led to dozens of small rooms.

I put down my bag and began rolling concussion grenades along the white vinyl hallway. The explosions were harmless, but the walls shook from the impact of each blast. Doors along the corridor opened suddenly, and beautiful women began emerging from the rooms. They were dressed in plush terrycloth robes, and their heads were wrapped in luxurious bath towels. All of them were frightened by the noise and smoke.

"Get out!" I yelled, pointing toward the lobby area. "You're free now, they can't make you stay here anymore!"

Some of the women looked dazed, but others began to move along in the direction I indicated. I knew that Poppy was conducting a similar evacuation on the other side of the building.

"You're Tina's brother!" yelled a statuesque blonde, grabbing me by the elbow. "She said you would get her out someday!"

"Our informants told me she's always confined in the President's office," I said. "Can you show me the way?"

The blonde led me farther along the corridor, and we ducked under a metal gate that was stamped with the words 'Authorized Personnel Only.' We continued down a narrow hallway, and finally she pointed toward a heavy wooden door.

"You go back," I said. "I can manage from here."

The door was locked, but I quickly attached a small plastic explosive charge to the knob. The blast sent splinters flying in all directions, and without hesitation I lunged into the room.

It was arranged like a doctor's office, with an examination table in the middle of the floor and rows of metal shelves against each wall. The shelves were crammed with clear glass jars, all of which were filled with varying amounts of thick white liquids.

"Skeeter!" screamed a voice, and then Tina raced out from her hiding place in a corner and threw her arms around me. "I knew it was you!" she said, sobbing. Her bathrobe felt damp, and her skin glistened under the lights.

And then I saw The Swine.

He was cowering behind his desk, glancing toward the door as if waiting for his chance to run away. He didn't have the guts to stand and fight. Tina pointed at him, disgusted, and hissed, "You will never get this close to me again for the rest of your un-natural life!"

The Swine stood up and thought about escaping, but I blocked his path to the door. "It's over!" I shouted. "Done! Finished! I know what goes on here. Using these women like test tubes, you and your insidious moisturizing experiments, splashing and smearing them with chemical mixtures day after day. No more! The Pond's Institute is closed!"

And with that, I took my aluminum bat and swung at a shelf full of glass jars. They shattered with an almost musical sound.

"No more stearic acid!" I exclaimed. "To hell with titanium dioxide! Goodbye, sorbitan oleate! Away with carbomer! Down with retinyl palmitate!" With each swing of the bat, another row of jars exploded, sending gobs of gelatinous white creams splashing onto the walls, floor, and ceiling.

The Swine started to cry. "All we're trying to do is reverse the aging process," he whimpered. "And without exploiting defenseless animals. Is that so bad?"

Tina ran over and slapped him on the face. The force of the blow knocked off his hairpiece and sent a full set of dentures flying out of his mouth.

160

"You see?" she said to me. "He's a complete fraud! A false human being!"

She tore open his shirt and ripped off the girdle he was wearing, and his blubbery stomach fell out over his belt. The Swine just stood there and took it, bawling like a baby. It was so pathetic, I almost felt a twinge of sympathy. Almost.

"We have to go," I said. "Poppy's waiting for us outside."

There was mass confusion in the corridor. Women were yelling with grateful excitement, and for the first time I noticed the presence of short, burly men wearing white lab coats. Tina saw my expression of curiosity. "Those are the lotion technicians," she said. "They're the ones who had skin-to-skin contact with us!"

"Hey, I recognize that one!" I said, grabbing the guy firmly by his collar. "You're Kent Drabbleford, from Paisley High School. We voted you 'Class Cow-Flop' two years in a row. I should have known you'd end up in a place like this."

"You think you're so high and mighty," he sneered. The little punk always had an abundance of cockiness. "Misfits like me made good money here, and we got to rub our hands all over beautiful girls in the process. These are jobs that can only happen under the free enterprise system. What am I supposed to do now? Enroll in some dipstick federal re-training program?"

He was pushed away by the crowd before I could answer. I led Tina back to the front entrance, and when we got outside I could see a parade of cars and vans coming up the road. Konrad was now lying on the ground beside our car, moaning incoherently.

"Did you call the police, or what?" Tina asked.

"Better than that," I said. "We tipped off local and national TV news bureaus," I said. "They'll serve as a distraction while we fly out of here."

"Fly? In what?"

"Look over there," I said, pointing to a grassy area behind the parking lot.

As planned, Poppy was standing beside a refurbished Bell UH-1H 'Huey' attack helicopter, waving at us vigorously. The pilot was an old family friend, a veteran of two wars and several medfly eradication programs. The blades of the chopper started to turn slowly as we ran toward it.

Some of the women had removed their bathrobes and set the pile of garments on fire. Smoke billowed into the sky as the captivating models danced in their lace undergarments, celebrating newly acquired freedom. Reporters were racing each other to get the first live, exclusive interviews. I saw a fistfight erupt between *60 Minutes* correspondent Mike Wallace and a crew from the Health & Fitness Channel.

"You are a sight!" Poppy exclaimed as we leaped into the cargo bay of the chopper. Suddenly we were airborne, and the scene below had a surreal quality as it grew smaller and began to recede in the distance behind us. "Honey, get away from the door," Poppy said, taking Tina by the arm. "Sit down. You can relax now."

"No!" Tina exclaimed. "I don't want to relax!" She leaned out and let the slipstream blow her hair into a mass of tangles.

"I want the hot wind against my face!" she said. "I want to feel my skin becoming dry and chapped! To have my pores clogged with dirt and oily residues! Let people guess my true age!"

We embraced again. She was sweating. And it was all right.

The Final Frontier

I eased back on the throttle, and the shuttlecraft settled gently down into a grassy field near a small housing subdivision.

"Nice landing, skipper," said Bendix, my co-pilot. "You think anybody on the ground saw us coming in?"

"They wouldn't even care," I said. "Listen up and I'll explain the situation." I unbuckled my shoulder harness and turned to face the passengers. There were forty-eight of them, seated in two long rows behind the cockpit.

"I can now reveal the purpose of this mission," I said. "All of you were handpicked because of your background in psychological counseling and mental health services. Our scout teams recently discovered that this planet has been culturally contaminated. Their normal societal development was distorted by an outside influence. And it was a deliberate act. The contamination came from one of our own people."

A woman raised her hand to speak. It was Science Officer Talia Deadmarsh, one of my former classmates at the space academy.

"I've heard rumors," she said, "that several planets in this region have been deliberately tampered with. And they say the culprit is still at large. Can you tell us anything about that?"

"As usual, the rumors are true," I admitted. "There's no use pretending otherwise. I suppose you also have a name for the person who's responsible for this interstellar crime spree?"

"Would it be Senator Montel Brady? The Mad Liberal?"

"Yes, but we didn't want you to know any of these details

until we got here. The press back home is having a feeding frenzy with this story, and we need to keep them off our trail right now.

"As most of you know, Senator Brady was the last surviving proponent of those discredited New Deal and Great Society programs of the mid-twentieth century. But his district, which was populated mainly by college professors, pacifists, failed writers, and over-the-hill performance artists, just kept re-electing him to the World Congress. When the term-limit rule was finally enacted, he was prevented from running for a 24th consecutive victory, and simply went out of his mind. It often happens to liberals who lose their political clout.

"Before anyone knew what he was planning, Senator Brady hijacked a hyper-drive star cruiser and disappeared. We've been tracking his whereabouts for the past fifteen years."

"What exactly is the nature of his cultural meddling on this planet?" asked Lieutenant Browser, one of my security guards.

"You're going to get a first-hand look," I said. "We're heading out on a field patrol immediately. Start your data collection as soon as we disembark the ship."

Leaving Bendix to guard the shuttle, I led our group down the exit ramp and proceeded on foot toward the houses a short distance away. We had been walking along a quiet street for only a few minutes when we encountered one of the local inhabitants. He was sitting on a curb, staring at a house across the street and strumming a guitar.

"What's that strange object on his head?" Lt. Browser asked.

"A Stetson," I said. "They were popular in America until about 2043, when global cooling made wide-brimmed hats obsolete."

The inhabitant didn't seem to be aware that our group was

observing him. His lips were quivering, and it appeared that he was on the verge of some kind of emotional collapse. Then he pointed across the street and broke into a song:

> I had myself a good wife.
> She put up with my wild life.
> But then the booze and gambling killed my
>   luck.
> The judge gave her my house,
> And she thinks I'm a louse.
> And her boyfriend drives a fancy brand of
>   truck!

"What in the world is *that* all about?" someone asked. Several members of our team were exchanging looks of dismay. I quickly pointed to the house across the street. There was a shiny red pickup in the driveway.

"He's upset because the female he covets is having relations right now with the owner of that internal combustion vehicle. He's using a song to express his pain and jealousy."

"The contamination!" Talia exclaimed. "Now I understand. It's country-and-western music!"

"Absolutely correct," I said. "Senator Brady apparently spent considerable time here disseminating a wide range of country tunes, and the planet is now suffering the consequences. This society was in the midst of a healthy industrial movement. Cities were growing, and factories were prospering when Brady arrived.

"Now the whole system is crippled by rampant alcohol abuse and lack of self-esteem throughout the population. These people have lost their ability to form lasting personal relationships, and the preferred method of intimate communication is writing lipstick letters on bathroom mirrors."

I could see many of the team members shaking their heads and scowling. Silently, our group continued up the street until we came to a second inhabitant. This person was standing on his front lawn twirling a rope with a huge loop in it.

"How goes it?" I inquired with a friendly wave. He responded with a scowl, and began singing:

> Well, I've eaten mud and I've tasted blood,
> And I've heard the roarin' crowds!
> I've held the reins and I've held my pain,
> So I wouldn't scream out loud!
>
> Well, there's broken bones and broken homes,
> And there's dreams that won't come true.
> But I wouldn't do a dang thing different,
> That's the life of a Buck-a-ROO!

I heard a strange yelping noise, and when I turned around I saw Lt. Browser cowering in fright behind a nearby clump of ornamental shrubbery. Talia and I walked over, grabbed him by the shoulders, and pulled him up to a standing position.

"Get yourself together, Lieutenant!" I ordered.

"Sorry, sir," he said, trying not to choke. "It's just that, well, I've never heard anything so disturbing in my life!"

"There are sedatives in your medical kits," I reminded everyone. "These songs *can* cause extreme mental disorientation and bewilderment, but your training at the space academy should pull you through any rough spots. As far as we can tell, Senator Brady distributed recordings by Garth Brooks, Rhett Akins, The Judds, Willie Nelson, Dolly Parton, and someone named Reba."

"I never heard of any of those people," Lt. Browser said. He was starting to sound like a whiner, and I was getting irritated.

"Never heard of them?" I snapped. "For God's sake, Lieutenant, what planet did you grow up on, anyway?"

"Altair-4," he said sheepishly. There was an embarrassed

silence, and I was sorry I had posed the question. Altair-4 was the only planet to be colonized entirely by Jehovah's Witnesses.

"Well, that explains a lot," I replied, making a mental note never to bring up the subject again.

"Skipper! Skipper!" It was Bendix, my co-pilot, running toward us from the direction of the shuttlecraft. I knew he wouldn't have left his post unless something serious had occurred.

"Coded message just came in from the Polaris," he said, panting from his exertion. The Polaris, our sister ship, was about forty million miles away, exploring the nearest neighboring planet.

"Bad news?" I queried.

"I'm afraid so. Polaris reports more contamination. The planet just beyond this one is populated by a race of intelligent three-legged dwarf humanoids. Senator Brady apparently gave them VCR technology and then indoctrinated them with a complete set of old *Star Trek* home videotapes."

"Oh no!" I shuddered. "Was it the 'classic' or 'next generation' series?"

"Both, unfortunately. Polaris says the inhabitants are now on the verge of a full scale civil war over whether Captain Picard was better than Captain Kirk."

"Was Kirk the one with the pointed ears?" Lt. Browser asked.

"Don't concern yourself with that," I said. "You're staying here, Lieutenant. I'm transferring you to the supervision of Science Officer Deadmarsh. She'll be a big help to your career."

"Thanks a lot," Talia said, with a hint of sarcasm.

"Everybody hear this," I said, gathering the team around me. "A support vessel will be here in a day or so. Then you can start whatever procedures are necessary to reverse this deplorable situation. I am proceeding immediately to assist the Polaris crew.

"If anything should happen to me, you must continue the search for Senator Brady. There is a particular phrase he uses to introduce himself on his planetary visits. It was popular among liberals in the old days. So when you find a new race of beings, you must test them by saying this phrase. And if they react in a positive way, you know they've been contacted by the Mad Liberal."

"And what is the test?" Talia asked.

"Ten terrible words," I said. "Ten words that can wreck any society: I'M FROM THE GOVERNMENT, AND I'M HERE TO HELP YOU."

Order of Importance

We had been on the mountain only six hours when the storm hit. "This looks real bad!" Joyce yelled as the first gust of powdery snow whipped in from the west. "Let's head back to those Forest Service cabins!"

There were two crude wooden huts at the edge of the treeline. It took us about ten minutes to hike down the icy slope to the nearest one. Old and dilapidated, it offered minimal shelter.

Freezing wind whistled through the cracked walls, and the visibility outside immediately dropped to zero.

"No need to panic," I said as we took off our day packs and huddled together. Joyce already knew what I was thinking, and quickly handed me the cellular phone. My hands were shivering as I punched in the numbers. The response was prompt.

"9-1-1 Emergency. This is Elaine, how can I help you?"

"Elaine," I said, "this is Albion LeBlanc, and I'm calling from the south face of Big Mountain. My friend Joyce Winslow and I were trying to hike up to the top when this storm blew in."

"Yeah, kind of a surprise for this to happen in July," Elaine said. "Did you pack an electronic radio locator?"

"We're activating it right now," I said, giving a thumbs-up sign to Joyce, who was holding the small black box in her hand. "Also, you'll be glad to know that I'm using the deluxe model, which transmits heart rate and blood pressure readings on a special sideband frequency."

"Okay," said Elaine, "I've got the signal coming in loud and clear on my display monitors. Are you sheltered?"

"We're inside an old cabin," I said, "but it's pretty flimsy. I'm not sure how long we can hold out in these conditions."

"Resources are being mobilized as we speak," Elaine said, "and I have put you on the rescue list. You're number 16."

"Did I hear correctly?" I replied, taken aback. "Am I to understand that 15 other people are in trouble up here?"

"No, 15 other *groups* of people," she said. "And those are just the ones we know about. Our top priority right now is a little boy on the east slope who has a terminal illness."

"What's a sick kid doing up here?" I wondered.

"It's one of those make-a-wish contests," Elaine said. "The boy wanted to climb Big Mountain, and he wrote the winning essay, so members of a local charitable foundation were hauling him up to the summit on a stretcher. But now they're all stuck in a small cave, and the group leader is running a high fever."

"Sounds pretty serious," I agreed. "Any idea how long the storm will last?"

"Not yet," Elaine said. "Give me your phone number and we'll keep you updated as we get more information."

By then, Joyce had unfolded our aluminized heat-reflecting ponchos, and we sat back-to-back for added warmth.

"If you don't mind," she said, "I'm just going to meditate for awhile. It's my preferred method for staying calm."

"Good idea," I said. "I'll be right here if you need anything." It was, I realized, a rather lame comment. Joyce pretended not to notice.

The phone rang about four hours later. "I hope this is good news," I said into the mouthpiece.

"I'm afraid not," said Elaine on the other end. "Weather forecasts indicate no letup in current conditions for at least the next forty-eight hours. And all of our available personnel are now trying to reach little Eddie, the sick boy in the cave."

"Surely you could spare a few people to help the rest of us," I said, somewhat testily.

"This is a bare-bones operation," Elaine replied. "Remember Ballot Measure 41, the property tax rollback that passed so resoundingly in the last election? The county had to downsize every department, and emergency services took a huge hit."

"Spare me the fiscal details," I said. "Can't you put out a call for volunteers? Tap into the community spirit?"

"The community wants to stay warm and dry inside their homes right now, while they enjoy those lower taxes," Elaine said. "However, I'll be glad to call your place of employment and tell them why you're not going to be on the job tomorrow."

"I guess that's better than nothing," I conceded. "We both work at First Income Capital Management Group."

"Oh, what a great company!" Elaine replied. "I'm in your Energy-Worldwide Growth Fund. I've already doubled my money." Since we seemed to be developing an efficient working relationship, I didn't tell Elaine that the Energy-Worldwide fund manager had just resigned to start his own investment group.

I must admit the temperature wasn't too uncomfortable once the snow piled up around the cabin and sealed us off from the howling wind. Lack of adequate light was my biggest concern, as my circadian rhythm is easily disrupted. Unfortunately, I fell into a sound sleep before I could inform Joyce about this condition.

After what seemed like a brief nap, I felt my head and shoulders being jostled. "Sorry," I said. "Must've dozed off."

"No kidding," Joyce said, pulling me up to a sitting position. "You've been unconscious all night. But I just heard a helicopter. Somebody must be coming to help us."

The sound of footsteps thudded across the sagging plywood roof, and a voice said, "Joyce and Albion! Are you in there?"

"Yes!" we shouted back.

As we watched, the blade of a portable jigsaw slid through a crack in the boards, and a small hole was quickly and expertly cut. Sunlight streamed in, and then a man's face peered down at us.

"Hey!" I said. "You're Alex Champion, from the Channel 6 Rapid Reaction News Team."

"We go where the news is happening!" Alex said smoothly. "Listen, there's been a slight break in the weather, so we're cruising the mountain with Chopper 6 to check on folks who've been trapped by the storm. The official rescue effort is still moving at a snail's pace, thanks to all the budget cutbacks."

"You're taking us out of here, right?" Joyce asked.

"No, we can't do that," Alex said. "Chopper 6 is filled with toys for little Eddie, all donated by concerned viewers. We're making a surprise delivery to boost his spirits. If the weather cooperates, we'll carry the whole thing live on the noon show."

"Any chance you could pick us up after you've unloaded all the toys?" I asked.

"You should be fine if you sit tight," Alex said, avoiding a direct answer. "The forecast says the snow will taper off later today, so the cabin won't be completely buried."

"Don't you even want to do a short interview with us?" I pleaded. "Then our friends in town could see we're okay."

"Let me ask you something," Alex said. "Are you two falling in love or anything like that? See where I'm going with this? Trapped together and discovering new feelings. That's a story." Joyce stared at me with a blank expression, as if she had just been struck on the head with a blunt object.

"No," I said, trying not to sound hostile. "It's cold and

dark, and we have to use one corner of this cabin as an open latrine. It's not the kind of setting that someone would pick for a budding romance, if you get my point."

"Too bad," replied Alex. "Please understand, there's nothing very unusual to report about your situation. I'll save my videotape for Eddie. The plight of a small, innocent child is definitely more compelling than a couple of healthy adults who made a stupid decision. Not that I'm being judgmental."

I got a bad feeling in the pit of my stomach as the sound of the helicopter drifted away into the distance.

"What a pompous oaf!" Joyce said. "I'll never watch that station again!"

"Should I have lied?" I wondered. "If he thought we were in here having a sex party, he might have helped us. But I just thought, you know, it was such a rude assumption."

"Oh yes, I agree," she said, but I could detect a touch of uncertainty in her voice. There was an awkward silence.

Another day went by. I was groggy when the phone rang, and surprised to hear a friend from work on the other end.

"Is everyone in the office getting worried?" I asked.

"No," said my friend, "but the accounting supervisor wants to know if you're going to count this as vacation or sick time."

"I hadn't really thought about it," I said. "How did you get this number, anyway?"

"The people at the 9-1-1 center gave it to us," my friend said. "They're getting pretty flustered over there. The woman I spoke with couldn't answer any of my questions, and she was crying by the time I hung up."

"Tell the accounting department I'll get back to them," I said. "We need to make some decisions here."

"So, how are you two getting it on? I mean, getting along?" my friend asked. "Sorry, Freudian slip."

"Is that what everyone in the office is thinking about?" I said. "Thanks for being so concerned about our survival."

Joyce was not pleased when I gave her the new details.

"The heck with getting rescued," she said. "Let's take our chances and start walking. This cabin is going to be totally disgusting pretty soon."

"Hold on," I said. "Maybe we just need to be more aggressive with the emergency services people." But when I called the number, an unfamiliar female voice said, "9-1-1. Whatta you want?"

"I'm trapped on the mountain," I said. "Where's Elaine?"

"She's filed a stress disability claim against the department, and is now on a temporary leave of absence," the woman said. "Do you need to leave a message for her?"

"I need someone who knows what they're doing to get up here and help us!" I yelled. "Your lack of action is making me angry!"

"Hold on," said the woman, "I'm routing you to our anger counseling line."

"Wait—!" But before I could argue, the batteries in the phone went dead. We hunkered down for one more night.

The next morning dawned clear and calm. I hoisted Joyce on my shoulders, and she had no trouble knocking one of the roof boards out for our escape. But I was surprised when other hands lifted her up through the opening.

"Perfect timing!" said a cheery voice. In another moment, I found myself standing amid a group of smiling senior citizens. Their blue acrylic jump suits all bore the familiar patch of the Silver Foxes, an outdoor club for the over-65 set. The group leader was a ruddy fellow named Brannigan.

"We've been cooling our heels in an old fire lookout station about a mile up the trail," he said. "Our group was number ten on the rescue list."

"So you've got a cell phone, too?"

"Oh, sure," Brannigan said. "I just talked with the 9-1-1 people an hour ago. They told us your phone had gone dead, so we decided to swing by and see if you wanted to stay put or come down with us. I should tell you that if you wait for help from one of the official rescue teams, the emergency services department will send you a bill for all their expenses."

"No way!" Joyce exclaimed. "When did that policy start?"

"They seem to be making it up as they go along," he replied.

"Does that mean little Eddie will have to pay, too?" I asked.

"Oh, didn't you get the lowdown on that?" Brannigan said, chuckling. "Turned out the kid wasn't sick at all. Some kinda hoax they were pulling, suckered the media and everybody. The reporters are running around like wild monkeys right now. You'll hear about it, believe me."

And he was right. Little Eddie and his disturbing parents made headlines for weeks.

Joyce came up to me a few days later and said, "Do you think we're abnormal? I mean, shouldn't two healthy people trapped in a little cabin have some natural urges toward each other?"

"Well, honestly, I didn't feel that way," I said. "But don't take it personally." She did, though. I could tell.

Nobody was very sympathetic. We didn't get any news coverage. And no tabloid or movie studio has offered a dime for our story.

Obviously the system let us down.

Precautionary Measures

I don't know how they timed their entrance so perfectly. I'm guessing they bugged the house in advance, so they'd know when I was in a prone position. The rays from the sunlamp felt warm and soothing on my back, and I was glad the alarm clock on the bedstand would keep me from falling asleep. But just as the bell chimed, and I was about to roll over, a heavy weight suddenly pressed down and pinned me to the bed.

"Relax, Larry," said a man's voice. "You're going to stay put for a little while."

I bent my head around and saw a man who could have been the ghost of actor Sebastian Cabot. He was sitting on my buttocks, puffing on a long-stemmed pipe. "This is a bit of a hazard," he said, clicking off the sunlamp. "Your skin doesn't need damage from the ultraviolet end of the spectrum."

"May I ask who the devil you are?" I said, attempting to struggle. But it was quite useless, and he was amused by my frustration. Then I saw two other men, dressed in plain gray suits, walk past us, heading purposefully toward the hallway that led into the back rooms of the house.

"Those are my associates, Byron and Theodore," the fat man said. Smoke curled out of his mouth while he spoke. "We work for an organization that is helping to produce a major event of great prestige and high entertainment value in this area next year."

I scoured my memory, trying to guess what he was talking about. "You mean the Olympics?" I asked. "Those aren't happening here. The closest venue is Bridgeport. That's fifty miles away, and all they're hosting is a first round women's field hockey match between Ivory Coast and Honduras."

"For security reasons," said the fat man, "I'm only allowed to refer to our production as The Event. But everyone connected with it is absolutely committed to the highest standards of public safety. We are determined to prevent any incident that might endanger patrons at The Event, or tarnish its reputation."

"What does this have to do with me?" I demanded.

"Precautionary measures are going to be extremely thorough," said the fat man, "and this is simply the first stage. House by house, we will make sure the entire area is safe for The Event."

"You think I'm a potential threat? That's ridiculous!"

"Larry," said the fat man calmly, "there's a method to all this. We're not chasing cats in the dark here."

One of the other men re-appeared, holding an electronic metal detector that I had purchased several years previously. "Whatta you suppose this is for?" he said with a smirk.

"Well done, Theodore," said the fat man. "Larry will surely enlighten us. How about it, old chum? Are you a seeker of buried treasure?"

"As a matter of fact, yes," I replied. "I go souvenir hunting with that device quite often, and I've found many valuable objects with it."

"I don't suppose," said the fat man, "that you've ever turned up an unexploded land mine, hand grenade, or other military ordnance that might be used to injure law-abiding citizens?"

"The most dangerous item I ever found was a rusty pocket knife," I said. "Seems unlikely there would be many land mines buried in the parks and public beaches where I hang out."

"Ah, the beach," said the fat man, blowing another cloud of smoke toward my face. "You know, Larry, I was once relaxing on the white sandy shores of the Cayman Islands when a man much like yourself actually bumped my head with the edge of his metal detector. It made me so angry I almost killed him, using only a small rock and a piece of string. So don't be insolent."

Theodore, still smirking, tossed my metal detector onto a nearby sofa and walked away.

"Is it possible for you to get off me for just a moment?" I asked. "My entire lower body is tingling because your weight is disrupting the blood circulation."

"Bear with us a while longer," the fat man said. "We should be finished here within moments."

"I can't believe you're going to sweep through every single residence in this area," I said. "It doesn't seem like an efficient use of your time and resources."

"We have lots of time, Larry," he replied. "And resources you can only dream about. No, we have this all under control, and you can rest assured that The Event will be conducted with absolutely no threat of danger or disruption. At least not from any human cause. I suppose we could still get hit by an asteroid, but that's somebody else's problem, not mine."

"If you were serious about this, you wouldn't be wasting your energy searching my place," I said, "you'd be down the street at Joe Griffey's house. Now *that* guy is a menace. He once came after me with his hedge clippers when I stopped by to solicit donations for the Children's Defense Fund. It was horrific."

"We've got him listed," the fat man said, nodding. "But we're starting with the easy targets first, so we can refine our techniques for the hard cases. Like Joe."

"I'm really in pain now," I said. "If you don't get off me for a moment, I think I may suffer permanent nerve damage. My legs have gone completely numb!"

"Let it not be said that I am taking sadistic pleasure in this," the fat man said, easing his bulk off my spine. The relief was so intense that I closed my eyes and let out a long sigh. Then, before I could take another breath, the weight quickly pressed back down on me.

"Hey!" I protested.

"Sorry, Larry," he said. "I was just shifting position. Your legs look fine, though. In fact, they have an attractive shapeliness that's almost feminine. Did you know that?"

"No," I said, trying not to groan. "Maybe I should pursue a career in female impersonation. I could be the next Betty Grable." I was truly angry now. I didn't care if my sarcasm offended him.

"I doubt that quite seriously," he replied coldly. "I knew the woman personally, Larry. And you are no Betty Grable."

"Look, boss!" said the other goon, Byron, bustling into the room with a shoebox in his hands.

"Be careful with that!" I snarled. "How dare you go snooping through my family heirlooms!"

The fat man stared into the shoebox and whistled softly.

"Well, how interesting," he said, picking up a piece of rusted, jagged metal. "Lots of odd fragments that appear to have been blown apart somehow. Is this one of your experiments, Larry?"

"For your information," I said, "those are pieces of the cannon shell that killed my great-great-grandfather at Shiloh. They were taken from his body by an army surgeon who was also one of his classmates at West Point."

180

"Gosh!" exclaimed Byron. "I don't have any of the bullet fragments that killed members of my family."

"How's Theodore doing?" the fat man asked. "Can we conclude this visit now?"

"I'm done!" Theodore's voice echoed from the hallway, and right then he popped back into the room. One cheek was bulging, and I realized he was eating an apple.

"These are great!" he said, holding up the uneaten portion. Then, while the apple dangled between his fingers, he leaned his head forward and took another bite. It was like watching a lazy horse nibble fruit from a tree.

"They're also expensive," I said. "Fruit-of-the-Month Club." Theodore was unimpressed, or didn't know what I was talking about, since his jaw continued its happy grinding motion without letup.

"Larry, it appears our work with you is finished," said the fat man. "Or, possibly, we are just getting started."

"I may need a doctor in either case," I said. I was certain my legs were turning black and would have to be amputated.

"A big job lies ahead of us," the fat man went on, "and we're always looking for new associates. I believe, from our brief engagement here, that you would be an excellent addition to the organization. Your lifestyle is not bizarre. The house is well kept. And you obviously know how to control your temper. These are all good attributes in our line of work."

"Are you making me a job offer?"

"It's part-time, but you'll get excellent benefits, and we have a meal allowance that's bigger than most third-world economies. In fact, right now we're heading to a four-star Italian place in Bridgeport. Care to join us?"

"Donna Emilia's?" I said. "That's supposed to be fabulous! But it's too expensive for me."

"Not anymore," said the fat man. He jumped off my back-side and landed on his feet with astonishing gracefulness. "By the way," he added, "when we get around to Joe Griffey's place, I'll let you have the honor of pinning his anti-social posterior to the floor while we inspect every nook and cranny of the house."

He held out his hand and then pulled me up to a sitting position on the tanning table. The pain in my legs was easing.

"I have only one concern," I said. "As a longtime follower of the naturist movement, I don't have an extensive wardrobe for working outside of my home."

"We can fix that."

"And what about The Event?" I continued. "Has anyone thought about making it clothing-optional? It might boost attendance."

The fat man stroked his beard, walked over to the phone on my desk, and picked up the receiver to make a call. "Larry," he said, smiling, "I think you just earned yourself a nice big raise."

End of the Grapevine

"He's out there on the patio," said the nurse, pointing toward a set of french doors that opened onto a small concrete slab. I could see a frail, elderly man hunched over in a wheelchair.

"Thanks very much for your help," I said, handing her a plain white envelope. She looked inside, saw the $50 bill, and nodded.

"He's on oxygen most of the time now," she said. "He may not last out the week."

"Is he alert?" I asked. "Can he hold a conversation?"

"Maybe, but not for more than fifteen minutes," she said. "Make it quick, and keep your voice down. We're not supposed to allow strangers to speak with the hospice patients. Why are you so interested in him, anyway? He's just an old dockworker."

"Sometimes people aren't what they seem," I answered.

The man sat with his hands clasped together, staring up at puffy clouds that billowed overhead in the spring sky. He regarded me with suspicion when I pulled up a chair beside him.

"Hello, Tom," I said softly. "I'd like to talk with you."

He took off the plastic oxygen mask and shook his head.

"Must be some mistake," he said. "I don't know you. And my name ain't Tom. It's George Ferguson."

"I believe otherwise," I said. "I think you're the man who once said, 'Wherever they's a fight so hungry people can eat, I'll be there. Wherever they's a cop beatin' up a guy, I'll be there. An' when our folks eat the stuff they raise an' live in the houses they build—why, I'll be there.' You remember those words, don't you?"

He looked away. A breeze wafted across the patio. Somewhere out in the garden a wind bell chimed softly.

"You covered your tracks pretty well, Mr. Joad," I continued. "I was beginning to think we might never have this conversation."

"So," he said uneasily, "you with the police?"

"Absolutely not," I assured him. "Private investigator. More of a researcher, actually. I work for the CCLC."

"Is that like the CIA? Spy stuff?"

"Not quite," I replied, "although very few people in the general public know about us. Our full name is the Coalition for Cinematic and Literary Closure. It's a non-profit foundation administered by a committee of university professors, the Writers Guild, and the American Movie Channel.

"For many years, readers and filmgoers in this country have been frustrated by well-known, prize-winning stories that have muddled, ambiguous conclusions. My job with CCLC is to track down people like you and find out the postscript. Nobody's looking for trouble. We're just hoping to tie up some loose ends."

"I guess it don't matter now," Tom said. "Even if you *were* a cop, I ain't gonna live long enough to go on trial."

"I assume you're talking about those guys who confronted you near the peach farm," I said. "One of them hit Casy, the preacher, with a pick handle, and then you grabbed the club and hit back."

"He killed Casy," Tom said, "so I gave him back a little of his own medicine. Been on the run ever since. I s'pose you heard all about what happened to Ma and the others. The car crash."

184

"Yes, we know that part," I said. "Summer of 1941. Highway 58 west of Bakersfield. A head-on collision with a Trailways bus."

"I was doin' field work not too far away, in Porterville," he said. "Read all about it in the paper. There was some kinda memorial service, but I stayed away. Figured the cops might be layin' for me if I showed."

"You probably would have died in that pileup too, if you had stayed with the family. Has that been difficult to live with?"

"Water over the dam," he said. "I stopped lookin' back the day we pulled outta Oklahoma. Past is past. Gotta look ahead."

"I understand," I said, taking a small notepad from my back pocket, "but I need you to look back, just this once. I want to know what paths Tom Joad has traveled all these many years, since *The Grapes of Wrath.*"

He put the mask over his nose and mouth and took several deep breaths. The sun dipped behind a cloud, and the wind suddenly felt almost chilly. The combination of oxygen and cool breeze seemed to invigorate Tom. His eyes opened wide, and he sat straight up.

"A fella I knew said we could find steady work farther up the valley," he began, "so we hopped a freight train and jumped off near Modesto. Found a nice work camp the local Salvation Army had set up, with showers and tents, kinda place where you could set for awhile and not worry 'bout gettin' run off by some posse.

"They give me a blanket and told me where to find an empty cot, but I got myself all mixed up and went into the wrong tent. The most beautiful girl I ever saw was sound asleep on an old dirty bedroll. And she was havin' some kinda bad dream, moanin' and shakin,' so I cleared my throat real loud and she woke up. Didn't seem scared of me at all. I says, 'Hello,

I'm Tom Joad.' And she says, 'Pleased to meet you. I'm Dorothy Gale."

"Dorothy Gale?!" I said, almost dropping the notepad. "From Kansas?"

"Yep, that's the one. I leaned over to shake hands, and her dog jumped up from under the covers and give me this souvenir." He held out his right hand, and I saw a long scar along the base of the thumb. "Sank his teeth right to the bone. Mean little son of a gun. Never let Dorothy outta his sight."

"What was she doing there?"

"Tryin' to get by, just like the rest of us," Tom said. "Her farm went bust. Not enough rain. Crops failed. The usual. She said Uncle Henry just keeled over when the sheriff gave 'em the eviction notice. Couple days later, Aunt Em ran outside during a big thunderstorm. They think she got hit by lightning."

"So Dorothy was all alone?" I asked, scribbling hurriedly.

"Oh no," Tom said, "I found that out real quick. Talkin' 'bout the family upset her, she started to cry, and right then someone grabbed me from behind, pinned my arms so I couldn't move, and knocked me in the head real hard. I went down, and when I rolled over I seen three guys staring at me. 'Mister,' one says, 'you get outta here and stay away from our girl.' They were farmhands from her place."

"Oh yes," I said. "Hunk, Hickory, and Zeke."

"They wasn't lookin' to make friends with anybody," Tom said. "And I sure didn't feel like fightin' all of 'em. I was kinda spooked, to be honest. It seemed like a real peculiar set up."

"Their relationship, you mean," I said.

"Right. It was . . . what's the word? Possessive. They wasn't lettin' anyone get close to that tent. But I talked to her a few times, on the sly, and she was smart as a whip. Wanted to get some land and be her own boss. I dunno how I got the nerve, but one day I said, 'Let's move on, just you and me.' And darned if she didn't say yes. She liked those farmhands, but she was scared of 'em."

"So you left the camp?"

"Yep. Headed for the Bay Area. I thought it'd be easier to lay low 'round a big city. Started calling myself George Ferguson."

"How'd you avoid getting drafted when the war broke out?"

"Flunked the physical," he said, chuckling. "When I got knocked down in Dorothy's tent, it ruptured an eardrum. So George Ferguson was 4-F, and those rejection papers gave me a new identity."

"What did you tell Dorothy? Was she aware of the incident with the pick handle?"

"We didn't keep secrets," Tom said. "I gave her the full story, and she was real good about it. Dorothy was no choir girl, ya know; she was a survivor. Her biggest problem was that knock on the head she got during the tornado in Kansas. And she was real insecure, but who could blame her? Losing the farm, her loved ones, it's gotta do some damage on the inside.

"Anyway, I got hired on at Hunter's Point shipyard in San Francisco. We found an apartment down the peninsula in San Carlos. Called ourselves George and Gale Ferguson. It all seemed pretty solid. But Dorothy, like I say, she'd have blue spells every so often. I couldn't talk to her. She'd just get weepy and start muttering, 'There's no place like home' and 'We've got to find the Emerald City!' And then after awhile, she'd snap out of it like nothing happened."

"Did you ever talk about getting married?"

"I tried," Tom said. "Told her we could take a bus to Reno some weekend and make it official. She wouldn't do it. I think the idea of settling down made her unsettled. So the longer we stayed together, the more restless she got. One day in 1944, she just took off. Middle of July. Couple of days later, I got a call from a policeman in Antioch, up in Contra Costa County. He said they was holding Gale Ferguson, and would I come and get her?"

"Dorothy had been arrested?"

"Not exactly," he said. "She'd been seen by a buncha people 'round town, shop owners who said she was carryin' on 'in strange ways,' whatever the hell that means. And she got sassy when a cop tried to ask her some questions, which ain't surprising. That girl could be a firecracker when she felt like somebody was pushing her.

"I borrowed a car and drove up there, and it was like a hornet's nest. People crowded 'round the jail, reporters, local folks, I don't know who-all was there."

"Because of Dorothy?"

"No, it turned out the Antioch police had another woman in the pokey, and she was being released that day. Frances Farmer."

"Frances Farmer, the actress?!" This time my notepad really did fall to the floor, and I didn't bother to pick it up.

"I heard they had picked her up for vagrancy," Tom continued, "and it was a lucky thing too, because nobody gave me so much as a second look while I was getting Dorothy outta the building. The only hitch was when they took me back to her cell. The dog poked its head through the bars and bit me on the ankle." He bent over and pulled down his right sock, revealing another livid scar.

"What a weird coincidence," I said. "Did Dorothy and Frances Farmer talk to each other while they were in custody?"

"Oh yeah," he said. "Frances told Dorothy she was bein'

railroaded by her parents in Seattle and a buncha other folks who thought she was too radical. She was in one helluva mess. I s'pose you know they stuck her in the loonie bin up there."

"Right," I said. "The Western Washington State Hospital at Steilacoom. That was a very controversial facility."

"I think 'snake pit' is more like it," Tom said. "The stories Frances told Dorothy, why, you wouldn't treat a wild dog so bad. But the inmates didn't have nobody on their side back then.

"After we got home, Dorothy was real upset for weeks. Bad nightmares. Sometimes she'd crawl 'round the apartment, sound asleep, yelling, 'How 'bout a little fire, scarecrow?!' And then she got it in her head that we should leave the Bay Area."

"And do what?" I asked.

"Move to Seattle. Frances told her 'bout growing up there, how beautiful it was. We argued a lot. I was doin' good at the shipyard, and I figgered California was gonna be booming even after the war ended. But she wouldn't change her mind, especially after she found out that Seattle's nickname is The Emerald City."

"It sounds like she was determined to go," I said.

"Yeah. I woke up one day in 1946 and she had her bags packed. I gave her money, and told her to call if she needed anything. But we both knew it was over. Dorothy just had a terrible hurt inside, and I couldn't heal it.

"I stayed busy so I wouldn't have time to think about her. Started up a yardwork business on weekends. Took some night school classes. Scraped up enough money to buy a duplex. And I didn't hear a word about Dorothy until 1949. Another phone call."

"The police?" I asked nervously.

"No," Tom said, "this one was from a reporter at the

Seattle *Post-Intelligencer*. She was doing a story, an exposé she called it, about the mental hospital where Frances Farmer was being held. She hadn't been able to speak with Frances, but one of the other patients she interviewed claimed to be my sister, Gale Ferguson, and was I aware of her situation?"

"Dorothy was in Steilacoom?!" My brain reeled. "Why?"

"She had got into some kinda trouble 'round town, sorta like what happened in Antioch," Tom said. "I suspect she mighta had one of her blue spells or somethin'. Anyway, the police decided she was off kilter and tossed her into the booby hatch. I'm not sure why she said I was her brother, unless she was tryin' to protect me. See, in those days a decent man wouldn't let his wife end up in the nut house, right? But if it's your crazy sister, well, that's different. Get my drift?"

"Very clearly," I said. "So, did you try to get her out?"

"I had a car by then, and I drove straight through. Took about sixteen hours. But it didn't matter. When I got there, she had just been released. I almost bumped into them out in the parking lot, but I ducked down so they didn't see me."

"Who?" I demanded. "Who was she with?"

"Hunk, Hickory, and Zeke," Tom said. "I about fainted. She musta stayed in touch with 'em even while we were together. They sure wasn't smart enough to find her on their own."

"That's incredible," I said. "Any notion where they went?"

"I thought about following them," Tom said, "but it woulda been wasted effort. I had to laugh, though. When they stopped to get into their car, Zeke tried to take the dog away from Dorothy, and it bit the bejesus outta his hand. Clamped on like a gila monster. He was squallin' like a baby. Big yellow-belly!"

"How do you sneak a pet into a psychiatric hospital?" I mused.

"Dorothy was amazing," Tom said. "Nothin' woulda surprised me with that girl. But like I said before, that knock on the head caused all kinda trouble. I can picture her wanderin' 'round that hospital sayin' 'There's no place like home' and 'If I only had a brain!' She's lucky they didn't put her away in a padded cell."

"So you just went back to the Bay Area?"

"Like I said before, past is past. You hafta let it go. I stuck with the shipyard work for enough years to get a longshoreman's pension. Even bought another duplex. I s'pose Ma and the others'd be surprised that I turned into a city boy. Too bad I didn't quit smoking a few years earlier. My lungs are payin' the price right now."

"Did you ever hear from Dorothy again?"

"Coupla times. She called me on the phone one night, I think it musta been 1966. Said she was passing through on her way over to the central valley, Delano I think, to help the farm workers with the grape boycott. I didn't ask her much about where she'd been. Didn't feel like it was any of my business, really."

He reached for the oxygen mask and placed it over his nose and mouth again, taking a few more deep breaths.

"Something I don't get," he went on, "is why you don't know a lotta this stuff about Dorothy already. You said your outfit is trackin' people down, tryin' to wrap up loose ends and such. Seems to me like somebody dropped the ball."

"I guess we just assumed the story was neatly resolved," I admitted, feeling completely embarrassed. "She got knocked out in her bedroom, had the dream about going to Oz and battling the wicked witch. And then she woke up and everything was fine."

"Hmph!" Tom snorted. "Good thing you decided to come down from your ivory tower and mingle with us hpeons at ground level."

He began to cough loudly then, gulping air and then gasping as his body shuddered. The nurse I had bribed opened one of the patio doors and leaned out. "You have to wrap this up," she said. "My supervisor will be here in a few minutes."

The coughing subsided, and Tom nodded at the nurse. She stepped back into the building, and I stood up to go.

"I sincerely thank you," I said, holding out my hand. He shook it firmly. "We now have closure on Tom Joad. And I've already started my next assignment."

"So you're gonna look for Dorothy?" Tom asked.

"We'll give it our best shot. You think I should check over around Delano first?"

"Nah," he said. "The last word I ever got from her was a postcard she sent me from Indianapolis."

"What do you suppose she was doing in that part of the country?" I wondered.

"Frances Farmer died there," Tom answered. "August of 1970. Dorothy musta been at the funeral. She could really get around." The nurse banged on the glass urgently.

"I guess that means I have to go," I said. "Thanks again."

"I'm not gonna last long," Tom said. "You knew that, right?" I nodded.

"Well," he continued, looking up at the milky clouds billowing overhead, "do me a favor. If you catch up with Dorothy someday, wouldja give her a message from me? Just tell her Tom said hello. And I hope she finally found a home."

"I'll do that," I promised. "You have my word."

"And one more thing," he added, holding up his scarred thumb. "Watch out for that damn dog!"